THE PROMISED LAND DIARIES

5

Songbird of the Nile

The Diary of Miriam's Best Friend

Egypt, 1527–1526 BC

BakerBooks
Grand Rapids, Michigan 49516

Diary One
The Land of Goshen
1527 BC

The Lake of Crocodiles

I'm trying to balance on the limb of a sycamore fig tree while I write, but it's not easy. If I slip, I'll fall into the lake that swirls below, a muddy soup of crocodiles and hippopotamuses. My best friend Miriam talked me into this. We are twelve years old and have been best friends for as long as I can remember.

She came by my house this morning and insisted that I come with her. "Hurry, Laila," she said. "The river is rising. We can watch it from a special spot I know."

I didn't know she was talking about the Lake of Crocodiles. Each year the crocodiles lumber up these sandy shores to lay their eggs. I was here one other time when I was a child, and it was with my father. I call him Av. I was small, and he carried me on his back like a sack of grain. He was quick and darted up a tree—like this one that I'm balanced on—so we could watch the spectacle below.

The huge beasts crawled up the soft banks and shoveled out holes with their wide, webbed feet. There were at least fifty crocodiles scattered across the southern shore, and they crouched over sandy nests until their eggs dropped inside. We were fortunate that none of the crocs crawled too close to the tree, Av said, and he warned me never to return here again.

Father is an engraver and not a shepherd, but many of the shepherds in Goshen have lost their livestock, or more, in the jaws of the crocodiles. Our good friend Becher is one of those men. Long ago, when he was young and inexperienced (he always emphasizes this point when he tells the story), he led his thirsty flock to a pool of water left by the receding river.

Becher didn't see the danger hidden in the tall grasses. A crocodile lunged forward and snatched one of his lambs between razor-sharp teeth. The lamb cried pitifully as the beast pulled it toward the river. Within seconds the croc had submerged the lamb beneath the water and begun his death roll.

Becher didn't hesitate. He jumped into the river to rescue the little animal. He startled the crocodile, and it loosened its grip on the poor lamb so that Becher was able to carry it to the shore. As his sandaled feet touched the wet banks, he felt a sharp pain and fell to the grass. He turned to see the crocodile swim away with his leg dangling from its jaws. A trail of blood floated on the surface of the water. His leg had been bitten off below the knee with one savage chomp.

Becher sold his flock after that. It was impossible to care for them with one good leg. He would not, however, part with his little lamb—a full-grown sheep now named Hoshaiah. That sheep follows his master everywhere. Becher is famous in Goshen because he's quite a sight. He hobbles along on wooden crutches tucked beneath his arms, and Hoshaiah follows him all the way. They walk together to the market, to the baker's shop for bread, and to the town gate to catch up on the day's gossip. They are never apart.

When Becher lost his livelihood, Father trained him to be an engraver. Today they are partners. They work side by side in the workshop in our house or at the marketplace. Mother (I call her Em) and Becher's wife, Atera, are friends. I'm fond of their daughter, Eva, though I don't see her often. She married not long ago and moved to another part of Goshen.

"Do you remember what the name Hoshaiah means?" Becher sometimes asks me.

"God has saved," I say and stroke the thick, coarse wool of the sheep's back.

"Don't ever forget that," he's told me numerous times. "God always hears the cries of his beloved children."

Egyptian fishermen have also lost their limbs and their lives to the crocodiles and the hippos. That's why they pray to Hapi, the god of the great river, who wears a crown of papyrus or lotus plants. They believe their prayers will keep them safe and will also cause the river to flood and water the crops. I've been trying to remember one I often hear, but it eludes me.

I just asked Miriam if she remembers what the prayer is. She's standing on a bough, gazing at the river to our left. She remembers details that I don't.

"There are several," she told me. "One goes like this: '*Offerings are made to thee, Oxen are slain to thee, Great festivals are kept for thee, Pure flames are offered to thee.*'"

Miriam sometimes sings her words as she did just now. I hope her beautiful voice floated on the river currents to Hapi's home in the caverns along the banks. Of course, our people don't believe in Hapi the river god, or in Re the sun god, or any of the other Egyptian gods. We worship only the God of our father Abraham.

This sycamore tree is ancient and quite tall. I stood up a moment ago and was surprised by how much I could see. The lake is slender like a canal. It slices through a wide valley and empties into an arm of Egypt's great river, Iteru. From where we sit we can see the two waters collide. The river slithers through the black land like a green snake. It's called the black land because the soil is dark and moist with the river's rich sediments. We live in the land of Goshen, which lies east of the river in the northern portion of the black land. Here the river's branches form a huge, watery fan.

Farther to the east are the granite mountains. When the sun rises, some people say they can see yellow gold glint from the mountains' veins. Kings from the north and south covet these mountains for their gold as well as the alabaster and precious stones hidden within.

To the west is the red land with its hills of shifting sand, the pyramids, the temple complexes, and the great sphinx. I think it's called the red land because the sand and the sun mingle at day's end to form a sea of rubies.

To the northeast I see the tall silos that store the pharaoh's corn and grain. They were originally built by Joseph, our forefather, son of Jacob. The white columns of the enormous store cities gleam in the sun. Egyptian hands as well as those of our own men are currently building these cities. It's part of Pharaoh's building project.

Oh, I'm losing my balance on this branch, and I must find another. I will return.

Moments Later

If I shade my eyes from the glare of the sun, I can see the faint line of the Wall of the Ruler far to the east. It's on the western border of Lake Sirbonis, which empties into the Egyptian Sea. No one can leave Egypt and travel eastward on the road of the Philistines without first passing through the wall. It's part of a garrison, or post where soldiers are stationed, that's under the command of a captain and guarded every minute by watchmen.

The Lake of Crocodiles cuts to the north and flows like a ribbon into the sea. If someone wanted to enter Egypt from the east and they were clever enough to get past the wall unnoticed, they would have to find a way to get across this crocodile-in-fested lake. If they didn't, they would be doomed to travel farther south into the wilderness. Even then it wouldn't be easy. Soldiers guard the north-south border of Egypt, and it's difficult to get in or out. Traders are the only ones with free access, but even they are questioned and their goods are scrutinized.

Some of our people in Goshen have begun to feel like trapped animals. They resent the way Pharaoh treats us. Others are grateful for the beautiful, bountiful country we live in, even if it isn't our own. I suppose I feel both ways.

The palace of the pharaoh twinkles like a jewel in an oasis. Miriam has already targeted it for our next adventure. We'll crawl down the river and hide among the reeds like stalking tigers, she tells me. This way we can spy on the palace and see if we can spot the king! He's rumored to have a beautiful daughter, though we've never seen her.

Life is always an adventure with Miriam. She's right about the rising river. The flood season is almost here, which means Iteru will overflow its banks. The Egyptians believe that once a year the goddess Isis sheds a tear into the upper Nile so it will flood.

It's a happy time and also a sad time for our people. A good flood brings a good harvest, which brings prosperity. Unfortunately, the work on the store cities is doubled after the river floods. Little can be done in the flood season, so Pharaoh thinks it's a perfect time to work harder on the building projects. Av is gone for several months during the flood season. He and the other men live in an encampment close to Pithom. Our people used to be free and happy to live in Goshen, but that was before the new pharaoh turned our men into slaves.

It's not nesting season, but Miriam and I still need to be careful when we climb down. Crocodiles are camouflaged among the river reeds, and they spring to life when someone walks near. Most of the time, they scurry into the river to escape. They aren't aggressive unless they're protecting their young, but I don't want to take any chances.

The orange sun is low in the sky. It's time to leave. I hope Av doesn't find out that I was here.

At Home

I returned a short while ago to a quiet house. It's a good thing I came back when I did. The bread was baking in the oven upstairs, but Av and Em were nowhere to be found. It's never happened before. Av sometimes returns late from the market—he never refuses a customer—but Em is here every evening at this time. She's fired the bread and prepared the supper every day for as long as I can remember.

Our kitchen is located upstairs above our bedroom, and it's where I sit now and wait for the bread to brown. There's no roof above me. It was built this way so the heat from the oven could escape and not stay trapped within our walls. Tonight it doesn't matter. The air outside is hot and humid, and my tunic is sticking to my back. The first star winked at me, but I'm too flustered to give it much thought.

I just heard a rustle downstairs and the sound of our heavy door opening and closing. Now I hear two pairs of footsteps. One walks with purpose, and the other runs and jumps. It isn't Mother and Father; Miriam just burst through the door with Aaron, her little brother of three years. I need to find out what's happened.

To Continue . . .

The mystery is solved. There was an emergency gathering at the home of Jochebed and Amram, Miriam's mother and father. Av and Em sent Miriam over to get me. Many of our friends are gathered there because Shiphrah and Puah, two of our midwives, have urgent news. Although they're Egyptians, they help us with the births of our babies.

We'll bring along Em's bread and stew and join everyone at Miriam's home. I'll be sure to write when I return.

Later That Night

I have returned. Av and Em are in their bedroom, which is next door to mine. I can hear their hushed voices, though I can't make out what they're saying. I do know that Mother is disturbed and Father has been trying to calm her all night. I'll tell you the story from where I left off earlier.

I walked with Miriam and Aaron to their house.

It's not far from my own home. We're fortunate to live in an area of Goshen where the houses are nice. They're not as large as those of the wealthy, but neither are they as small as those of the poor. Most of the homes in our part of town are made of mud bricks and stand two stories tall.

"You don't have any idea what's going on?" I asked Miriam. We walked side by side on a dirt path. Aaron knew the way and was running well ahead of us.

"No, but I know it's serious," Miriam replied. "Shiphrah and Puah looked like they could cry."

We passed Becher's home. Atera was sweeping out the hall with a broom, and a cloud of dust and pebbles flew through the door. "Oh, hello, girls!" she called to us and waved. "Tell your mothers I will pray. Don't worry. *El Shaddai* is all powerful. He will take care of us in our hour of need."

Miriam looked at me. "Our hour of need?" she repeated. We waved back to her, but Atera had disappeared in another puff of dust. We heard her cough as we quickened our pace. Atera is a godly woman who can be counted on to pray for our people and our homes. If ever there is a problem, she's the first to know about it and the first to pray.

At least thirty people were gathered in the reception hall of Miriam's home. It's not a large room, but it's the one used to receive guests. Some were seated in chairs or along the clay dais that ran along the wall. Most were standing. Shiphrah and Puah stood in the front of the room beside their hosts, Jochebed and Amram.

I was relieved to spot Av and Em. Becher was there too, as well as many of our close neighbors and friends.

"Tell us again, please," pleaded a woman called Bernice. "I'm sure we must have misunderstood." Her belly was large and round, and she held both of her hands over it in a protective fashion. It was clear that she was with child. Tears streamed down her cheeks, and her husband cradled her head against his chest.

Shiphrah shook her head. Despite her advanced age, her hair was dark and shiny; only a few streaks of gray coursed through it. "I'm afraid you've not misunderstood," she said. "Yesterday we [she inclined her head toward Puah] were called to the king's palace. These were his exact words to us: 'When you help the Hebrew women in childbirth and observe them on the delivery stool, if it is boy, kill him; but if it is a girl, let her live.'"

There were many gasps in the crowd, and Bernice went limp. She collapsed into her husband's arms. Puah rushed forward and helped her to the floor. Miriam's mother ran to the kitchen and returned with a rag soaked in water. She handed it to Puah, who placed it over Bernice's forehead.

Then Puah stood and returned to the front of the room. Her hair, unlike Shiphrah's, was white. I was surprised that it didn't make her look old, but her black eyes were lively, and her face still held traces of the beautiful woman she'd once been.

"We have not come to frighten you." She spoke above the murmurs of those gathered. "We will not do as Pharaoh asked, but you must not breathe a word of our promise to you once you leave this house. If we are sentenced to death as a result of our disobedience, then so be it. We will not kill your innocent sons."

Shiphrah nodded her head in agreement. "We are called by the gods to help bring life into this world. We are not called to take it."

Miriam had been silent beside me until then. "This is a terrible thing," she whispered. "Terrible. It won't stop here. I hope you know that."

"What do you mean?" I asked her. I felt weak and tired. I still couldn't believe what I'd just heard.

"Shh! Listen."

Bernice's husband stood up. "Well, if you don't act as the king's henchmen, will there be others who will? Is he determined to take our sons at all costs?"

Amram held up his hand. "These poor women are not qualified to answer your questions, Elias. The new pharaoh is not like the ones of the past. He isn't Joseph's pharaoh, and he isn't like his predecessor. He's afraid of us."

"Afraid?" cried a woman whose name I didn't know. "Afraid of the innocents? What kind of a king fears the innocents?"

"It's not the babies he's afraid of," Amram explained. "It's our boys who will grow up to be men. It's *us*. The number of the Hebrews increases every year. When Jacob entered Egypt, there were only seventy. Now we number in the hundreds of thousands. Pharaoh fears that one day we will grow so numerous, we will usurp his authority. That's why we are in bondage in the mud pits."

Amram paused for a moment. "That's not all. There's something else you should be made aware of." He did a quick study of each of the faces in the room. All eyes were glued to him, waiting for him to speak. Amram is a noble man and well respected. Our people regard him as a pillar of strength and wisdom. He continued, "A certain scribe, whom the pharaoh believes talented and reliable in foretelling future events, predicted that a child would soon be born to us—"

Elias interrupted. "This is your news, Amram? As you can see by my own wife, many children will be born to us. Every day in Goshen, children are born—"

"Let me finish, Elias," Amram said. His voice was quiet but full of authority, and it silenced the young husband. "This child, if allowed to live and grow, will be the one God has chosen to raise up our people and subdue the dominion of the Egyptians. He will be good and virtuous and one day obtain such glory, he will be remembered throughout the ages. It was this prophecy that frightened Pharaoh and preceded his order. If we try to protect our sons in any way, he has promised to destroy us as well. In answer to your original question, Elias, none of us is safe anymore, least of all our sons. Come and sup with us, and then go home and pray. We are in need of the Lord's divine protection."

This was the urgent news that had caused Em to leave the bread baking in the oven. Surely, I will never forget this day. I wanted to talk with Mother and Father about all of this, but there was no time tonight. Em was too disturbed and Av too weary.

Father promised to set aside time for me in the morning. I want to discuss the events before I talk with Miriam again. I already know how she feels. She thinks it's the beginning of the end for our people in Egypt, but if that's true, what then? What will become of us?

The Morning Watch

I awoke this morning to an eerie silence. Not just in our house but everywhere. Even the wild dogs are not barking. Is it just my mood, or do the magpies sing a melancholy tune in the willows outside my window? I'm sure most of Goshen has heard the terrible news by now. The depths of their sorrow must be great, for my own heart is heavy and dark.

Av led me to his workroom in the back of the house. He wanted to talk with me before Becher arrived. I love to linger in his workshop, and I often do when he's at the market. He even allows me to sit beside him on a wooden stool as long as I'm quiet and don't disturb him.

There is one long table, which catches my eye each time I enter. I never know what treasures I'll see there. This morning there were long slabs of limestone, chunks of milky quartz, clear crystal, and smooth mounds of brownish-orange clay. When Becher arrives, his expert hands will carve these into seals in the shape of cylinders, cones, or scarabs. Since the scarab beetle is sacred in Egypt, Av sells a large number of seals in the shape of the scarab to his Egyptian customers.

After the seals are carved, Av and Becher carry them to the marketplace. A customer brings in a copy of his signature, usually a small drawing, and Father uses special bronze engraving tools to etch the design into the seal. This becomes the man's signature, and most men have one.

The seal is most often attached to a cord and worn around the neck or around the waist. Sometimes it's worn on the finger of the right hand, but that's a special order, which takes more time. Becher uses metal to make the ring, and it's not unusual for the seal to be carved from precious stones like turquoise or rubies. The bearers of these special seals are usually palace officials, and they pay Av and Becher well.

When a man wants to use his seal to imprint his signature, he pushes it into a bit of soft clay and then attaches the clay to a document. If the seal is a round cylinder, he rolls it from one end of the clay to the other, and a series of signatures appears in the clay. Seals can also be dipped into ink and pressed onto paper, although that isn't the common way in Egypt.

Av rubbed his eyes and smiled at me. He pushed his tools into a corner and beckoned me to stand close. He drew a long line in the shape of a sloping hill in the dust on the table. At the base of the hill on the right side, he drew a dot with the tip of his finger. "This is where our father Abraham and his father, Terah, came from."

He drew an arrow to the top of the hill and over to the middle of the left side. "But this is where Yahweh called him to live." As he spoke, he drew a wide circle. "Yahweh promised this land to Abraham and his descendants. That's us, Laila, and every Hebrew who dwells in Goshen."

He drew one more line past the base of the left side of the hill and pressed another dot into the dust. "This is where we live now, in Egypt. It's a country that doesn't belong to us. We were meant to come here for a time, but we won't stay forever. Egypt was good to us for many years, but now it is a furnace of affliction. In the Lord's time, he will lead us back to our home—back to the Promised Land."

Av's words stirred me. Miriam has told me this same thing many times before. I suppose it's her father who told her. I should be happy when I think of our people returning to the land God promised them, but I feel torn. Egypt is my home. It's the only home I've ever known, and I love it. On the other hand, I must confess to terrible thoughts of the king, thoughts I'm ashamed of. I feel hatred for the first time, and I don't like this feeling.

"We must pray for the pharaoh, Laila," Av told me. "It will do us no good to fill our hearts with anger and hatred. It is he who will suffer at the Lord's hand one day." Had Father read my mind?

"But the baby boys," I lamented. "What will become of the babies?"

"I don't know," he admitted. "Those born right now will be safe. Shiphrah and Puah will see to that. We have no choice but to take one day at a time and trust in our Lord."

"Do you think it's true, Father, what the scribe prophesied to the king?" I asked. "That a baby will be born to us who will lead us out of our bondage?"

Av nodded. "These scribes, while they do not serve our God, are nonetheless very wise. They have made predictions time and again that have come to pass. They read the stars, and God allows them to see bits and pieces of his plans. Yes, Laila, I do believe a child will be born to us whom God will raise up to be our strong leader. I do believe it."

I left just as Becher hobbled in with Hoshaiah. He had a smile on his face and was about to greet me with his customary words—"Laila! You are more beautiful today than the last time I saw you!"

Father's voice, however, took his words away—"If you feed that sheep any more, my friend, he won't be able to fit through the door."

"Aw!" Becher growled. "I will feed this sheep whatever this sheep wants, because he is so devoted to me. What concern is it of yours if my Hoshaiah fits through the door?"

I don't know how Av and Becher can work together the way they argue. They've been best friends for a long time, but like Em says, they go at it like two old women.

I walked away with a smile on my face as I listened to their banter. After a time, they settled down. Quiet ruled the house as they worked peaceably side by side. I'm glad I spent time with my dear Av, but I can't say I feel much better. There's a sense of dread that gnaws at me when I think about the coming days.

One Week Later

What a relief! I can share at least one piece of joyful news. Bernice, the woman with child who fainted at Miriam's house last week, just gave birth to a baby girl. I felt happy for her and her husband, but Em didn't share my enthusiasm. "Isn't it a sad time, Laila, when we welcome the births of our daughters and fear the births of our sons?"

She's right. I walked with her to the rising river to gather several jugs of fresh water. We stood for a moment and watched the activity, although we were both absorbed in our thoughts.

A man stood on the bank near us and worked his water-lifting machine called a *shadoof*. The long pole was weighted on one end with a huge stone. On the other end of the pole was a bucket. He lowered the bucket into the water, and when it was filled, the weight of the stone lifted the heavy vessel out of the river with ease. All the man had to do was swing the pole around and either lift the bucket or pour it into a larger vessel. He was no doubt carrying the water away from the river to water his crops.

Two fishermen were in the river's middle with their papyrus boat. I take great pleasure in watching their interesting tactics. One of them slaps the water repeatedly with the oar while the other holds a net overboard and tries to snare the frightened fish. But today my heart was too heavy for me to laugh as usual.

A wooden river barge loaded with huge cubes of granite floated downstream from the rock quarries to the building sites. Sometimes, at the widest parts of the river, two barges float downstream side by side. One stone obelisk, shaped like a miniature pyramid, is so enormous and heavy that it must be carried on the backs of both.

Since Iteru flows north, the boats traveling downstream can use oars, and they are aided by the current. The boats traveling south use sails and are aided by the wind, which blows from the north.

"A few more weeks, and the flood will be upon us," Em murmured. We dipped our jugs into the water until they were heavy. Several huge mosquitoes darted around my face, and I let go of the jug by mistake as I tried to bat them away.

"Oh!" I cried. I reached for the clay vessel, but

Mother grabbed a handful of my tunic and pulled me back. We watched the jug bounce in the current, half submerged in the tepid water.

I was surprised at the tears that filled my eyes, and Em was too. She pulled me close to her, and before I knew it the salty drops spilled onto my cheeks. "It's just a jug, Laila," she said. "You are emotional. We all are. Remember, things can be replaced, but people can't. Come. We have enough water for now."

Two Days Later ~ Sunset

I have just returned from my adventure with Miriam. What a day it's been. She arrived at my door not long past sunup. I heard her singing with the magpies moments before and knew she was skipping down the road, kicking up dust in her usual manner. I opened the door just as her knuckles were poised to rap on the frame.

She smiled with such sweetness, I couldn't help but laugh. "Come on," she said. "We're going on a grand adventure."

"Now?" I asked. My hair wasn't even brushed.

"Now," she replied firmly.

Em peeked around the corner, and Miriam saw her. "That is, if you have completed all of your chores."

Mother smiled at this. Miriam might as well be a part of my family for all the time she spends here and how well she's loved.

"Go on, you two," Em said. "Laila, you've sulked around the house long enough. Have fun, but don't get into your usual mischief."

I ran a brush through my hair and let it hang loose down my back. Miriam had done the same, but her hair is smooth and silky. Mine is wavy and thick and always gets in my way. I wrapped a yellow ribbon around my forehead and tied it behind my head. It looks pretty, but mostly it helps keep my hair in place.

We walked out the door, and Miriam stopped to pick up a pole that was leaning against the tree. She balanced it over her shoulder and held the front end with her right hand. A large sack was tied to the other end, and it dangled behind her.

"I've packed us a lunch so we can have a picnic. We can take turns carrying it."

She had already skipped ahead, so I ran to catch up.

"You haven't even told me where we're going," I reminded her.

"To Pharaoh's palace! I told you that would be our next adventure. Don't you remember?"

I had forgotten. What felt like a grand adventure several weeks ago seemed like a bad idea now. I turned on my heel and walked back toward home. This time it was Miriam's turn to run and catch up with me. "Wait! What are you doing?" she called.

"I'm not going," I told her.

"Why?" she cried. "I thought you wanted to see it."

"*Miriam!*" I didn't mean to shout, but her startled eyes confirmed that I had. "How can you want to go there now? That king is wicked. Look at what he's doing to our people. Look at what he wants to do to our babies." My eyes were watering again, and I turned away, embarrassed.

I heard her set the pole down, and she stepped up behind me. She reached for my hand and tugged on it until I turned around to face her.

"Please try to understand." Her voice was quiet but urgent. "I know the king is wicked, but I need to go there. I have to see it, and I can't really explain why. I don't understand it myself."

I've known Miriam my whole life, but I've never seen her like this before. There was something there she had to see, and I don't think even she knew what it was.

"All right," I nodded, resigned. "If I don't go with you, you're going to go anyway, I suppose."

"Probably," she answered with a grateful smile. She picked up the pole and draped one arm around my shoulders.

We walked side by side. "I'm not like you, Miriam," I reminded her. "You're adventurous and bold. I'm quiet, and I'm afraid of things sometimes. I wish I were more like you."

Miriam grabbed my hand as she often did. "But that's why we make a perfect team! Father tells me I'm too headstrong. He says I should follow your example. I should be quieter and more thoughtful. I should think before I act."

I looked at her. "Your father said that?"

"Yes. Mother and Father admire you. They don't worry about me as long as I'm with you, because they know you're sensible!"

"I'm far too serious," I replied.

"I know," she laughed. "That's why you have me. Now, come on!"

That was how our adventure began, but the rest will have to wait. My hand must rest.

Later . . .

Our strides were quick at first, fueled with the excitement of a new adventure. I put my sad thoughts behind me as we followed an arm of the river north toward Avaris. There's a narrow piece of land called the floodplain on either side of the river. When Iteru overflows, this strip of land is flooded and later cultivated for crops. It's the most fertile soil anywhere. All of the homes are built just above it.

We passed small houses made of mud brick. This is the area where the poorer people live. Their homes are only one story with four rooms, although the very poor have only one or two rooms. Straw sleeping mats were hung out to air. They were strewn lopsided over the sides of the flat roofs.

Most of the people here sleep on their roofs at night. It's not just because they want air and it's too hot to sleep inside; there's no room indoors to slumber. Their tiny homes are filled with too many children.

I've been in many of these houses with Em. When word gets out that someone is ill, all of our people, whether rich or poor, try to help one another. Em and I bake bread and nutritious porridge at least once during each new moon. We take it to the old or the sick, whoever can't care for themselves.

I count all the good things I've received and say a small prayer of thanks to the Lord every time I come here. I'm thankful that Av is an engraver and that his work isn't dependent on the flooding of the Nile to ensure prosperity. Mother says we're blessed, because he has always been healthy and he's never missed a day of work.

The earth was dry, even close to the river's edge, and the air was hot. It's a sure sign that flood season will arrive soon. If we don't have a good flood this year, there are rumors that a famine will descend on Egypt like a hungry lion. The flood last year was not as good as everyone had hoped, so the harvest wasn't abundant.

We walked for several hours. When we were thirsty, we bent down at the shore and scooped up the water with our cupped hands. I felt gladness in my heart when Miriam's tireless energy and enthusiasm began to wane. It meant she was hungry, and that meant we could stop to eat lunch.

A wide jacaranda tree, heavy with lavender blossoms, was just ahead, and I was relieved when Miriam moved toward it. The pole was hoisted over my shoulder now, and the wood was growing heavier and heavier. It dug into my skin like a weighty yoke. Even when I switched it from shoulder to shoulder, as I had been for the past hour, there was no relief.

"Let's stop and eat. It's farther than I thought," Miriam said. We unwrapped the lunch and spread the cloth on the ground. It was wide enough for us to sit on as well as lay out our feast. With pride Miriam set out cheese curds, dates, crusty wheat bread, and thick layers of sweet, juicy onion.

This drew the attention of three guinea fowl that were watching us from afar. I laughed at them, as I always did. These birds have tiny heads with a bony protrusion on top, skinny necks, speckled feathers, and plump bodies! They're cute and odd all at once.

We ate everything except the crumbs, and then I lay back and rested my head on my entwined hands. If it weren't for the feeling of trepidation I've carried with me since the meeting with Shiphrah and Puah, the day would have been perfect. The sky was milky blue, and a light wind shook the purple petals above us. The branches provided shade from the sun.

We turned on our sides and watched a black scarab beetle near the blanket. It pushed a round ball of dung at least four times its size until it disappeared beneath the plant covering. No doubt its burrow was somewhere near.

The Egyptians believe the dung beetle is just like their god Khepri who pushes the ball of fire across the sky to make the sunrise. Khepri is one of the creator gods they worship, and he is said to have the body of a man and the head of the scarab beetle.

"I'm so glad our God doesn't look like that beetle," I mused out loud.

Miriam laughed. "Me too!"

We shook the cloth so that the crumbs flew into the air toward the guinea fowl. I tied the cloth onto the end of the pole, held it upright, and decided to use it as a walking stick. Miriam said it looked like I was marching into battle with my regiment's flag.

A short while later we saw the columns of the palace. The sun creates an interesting phenomenon. Depending upon the time of day when its rays bathe the limestone, the palace appears to be different colors. When Miriam and I viewed it from the sycamore fig tree above the Lake of

Crocodiles, it was so white, it dazzled. Now the same columns appeared gold.

We moved closer to the river reeds to conceal ourselves. Miriam was in front of me, and I saw her shoulder muscles tense and her steps slow down. Her breath was shallow.

There was a sudden flutter beside us. We swung our heads to look just as a Sacred Ibis flew from the cover of the thick bulrush and skimmed past our heads. Miriam jumped back and fell into me. We landed so near the water's edge, we could have rolled over and taken a swim.

This was the first time I'd been so close to a Sacred Ibis. It was much larger than I realized, at least three times the length of my forearm. Its body was white except for its black head and a tuft of black tail feathers. A long, curved black bill passed within inches of my head as the bird skimmed out over the surface of the river. It stretched its narrow head in front, and its long legs trailed behind it like an afterthought.

Miriam clutched my hand in her own. "Laila,

the Sacred Ibis is a holy bird to the Egyptians. It represents wisdom and knowledge and writing."

"Yes," I told her. "I remember that."

"Don't you see?" Miriam exclaimed. "There's a reason why we came here today. There's a reason why that bird appeared. The Lord can use nature and many things in our world to speak to us. We live in a time of great change, and we must remember everything. The Lord gives us all special gifts, and writing is one of yours. When we go home, you must chronicle our day."

If it's true that God gave me a gift to write—or better yet, to record—then he must have given Miriam a special gift of knowledge. It's because of her that I decided to keep a diary in the first place.

Much Later . . .

We crept close to the river and crouched low among the tall grasses. A grove of eucalyptus and tamarisk trees provided the perfect place to hide.

It was close enough to the palace to spy but far enough away that we couldn't be seen.

The palace is built on a slope, so it was easy to see from below. The tall, wide columns looked like papyrus stalks topped with lotus blossoms. Egyptian symbols were engraved into the stone pillars. One looked like an Ibis, similar to the one we saw earlier, only this one had a round black circle floating above it. Another symbol looked like a man, maybe an Egyptian priest, with his arms outstretched; yet another looked like a bird with the head of a man.

Another symbol was carved above the entrance: a large circle painted red to represent the sun. A pair of deep green wings extended outward out from each side of the circle. I've seen this symbol many times, and I remember asking Em about it years ago. She told me it's referred to as "the winged disc" and it represents one of the Egyptian sun gods.

Flower-lined paths wound from the terrace to the royal landing place at the river, but the king's boat wasn't in the kiosk, the small, wall-less structure that houses the king's fleet. A shallow bathing pool also flowed from the portico, which is a bathing floor and entrance to the river. The pool was separated by a low wall carved with lotus and papyrus plants, which seemed to erupt from the water.

One of the many palace gardens and courtyards was adjacent to the portico. There was a magnificent fountain in the center. A tall stream of water sprouted from it and bubbled into a pool of water. Date palms and a grove of fruit trees fanned their leaves in the warm breeze. I recognized the trees by their scents: orange, citron, plum, mulberry, apricot.

Miriam and I were speechless. It was beautiful and luxurious. Grape vines and deep-green ivy coiled around wooden poles and draped over the low walls. Daisies, cornflowers, mandrakes, and roses bloomed in shades of red, violet, blue, pale yellow, and dusty pink.

I had heard of painted floors and golden thrones, but we couldn't see those. As we watched, a tall woman came from behind the fountain and sat down on the ledge beside it. Her posture was so straight, I thought she could easily carry a plate of fruit on top of her head.

I heard Miriam catch her breath. "It's her. It's the princess," she sputtered.

The princess was dressed in a white linen sheath that fell to her bare feet in pleated folds. A matching shawl covered the tops of her arms. Her black hair fell to her shoulders in a straight, even line, and her bangs were worn short and straight across her forehead. The jewels of her headband flashed in the sunlight. Even from a distance I could tell that her eyes were painted in the Egyptian fashion.

The princess dipped her hand into the fountain and ran it back and forth in the water in a dreamy fashion. I thought she was beautiful, and Miriam agreed. I can't imagine what it's like to live in such a grand place and to wear clothes as beautiful as hers.

We heard a deep, guttural voice call to her, and she got up and disappeared behind the fountain.

We waited for a long while beneath the trees, but she didn't appear again.

"Come on," I told Miriam. "We should go. It's a long walk back."

We crept among the grasses close to the water's edge until we were at a safe distance from the palace. Then we were free to stand up and walk again. "Did you see what you wanted to see?" I asked Miriam. She was far away, lost in her thoughts.

"I think so," she said. "The princess seems like a kind woman, and for some reason that has given me peace."

We arrived home from our grand adventure just as the sun melted into the night

Just Past Daybreak

I was awakened to the sound of Av sharpening his tools, but I wasn't ready to climb from my bed. My legs ached from our long walk, and my mind was still dreamy with thoughts of the palace and the princess.

I wandered into Father's workshop without bothering to tidy my hair. It hung in messy waves around my shoulders, and Father laughed when he saw me. He drew me to him and hugged me tight before he continued with his work.

More than a dozen bronze chisels and a hand files of different sizes awaited their turn to be sharpened. I picked up several of them and examined their edges. They were worn and dull. Many more were stacked neatly in a wooden box. These were the ones that had already been sharpened.

Father dipped a rag into a bowl of olive oil and rubbed a thin layer on the hard, fine-grained surface of a large whetstone. The coarse side of the stone is used for the initial sharpening. He picked up a chisel, held it at an angle against the stone, and drew it with a firm hand along the surface. He did this several times, pausing to examine it every now and then until his expert eye was satisfied that both sides were sharpened evenly. Then he turned the whetstone over to reveal the polished side, and he drew the chisel along to hone and smooth the edges.

Em was already gone by the time I awoke. She and Jochebed have been busy tending to the families of newborns. In the weeks since Pharaoh's order, I haven't seen her as often as I used to. The families of infant boys try to keep their sons hidden in their homes. Since the mothers can't get around like they used to, Mother, Jochebed, Atera, and others check on them and bring them what they need.

Em left out a loaf of bread and bit of cheese. For the next few hours, the house will be filled with the music of metal grinding against stone. I think I'll go and visit Miriam!

An Order from the King ~ One Day Later

There was another gathering at the home of Amram and Jochebed earlier this evening. Once again our Egyptian midwives, Shiphrah and Puah, stood at the front of the room with their hosts. Many of the women were absent, hidden in their homes with their newborn sons. Their husbands came instead.

Everyone knew at once that the news wasn't good; Shiphrah's and Puah's faces were grim, even more so than last time.

Shiphrah spoke first. "As expected, we were called before the king. He demanded to know why we have allowed your boys to live. We gave him an answer that is true. We told him Hebrew women are not like the Egyptian women; they are vigorous and give birth before the midwives arrive."

Puah nodded. "I can attest to the truth of this. Your god has been with your women. We've not assisted in one birth since we met with you last, nor have any of the other midwives beneath us."

"But you've come to deliver more news," Av remarked. "That's why you've called us here. Am I correct to make this assumption?"

"You are," Puah admitted. "You will know soon enough, but we wanted to be the ones to tell you first. It's not good news, I'm afraid. By this time tomorrow, all people in Egypt will be ordered to report the birth or whereabouts of your infant boys. They are to be taken to the officials, who are charged with drowning them in the river. There will be severe consequences for those who know about the birth of one of your sons but withhold the information."

Mother, Father, and I walked home in silence. Becher and Atera walked in front of us, trailed by Hoshaiah. Only the sound of our footsteps on the dirt, the creak of Becher's crutches, and our heavy sighs filled the air.

I kept thinking about the Iteru I love. It's the river of life to Egypt. Is it now the river of death to our people? I squeezed Em's hand, and she bent down and kissed the top of my head.

I asked Av when we returned why Pharaoh would want to throw the babies in the river. Murder in any manner is cruel, but why drown innocent babies in the river, of all things? He reminded me that each year, at the start of the flood, sacrifices are made to the river gods. Pharaoh intended to use our babies as offerings to Hapi this year.

"The Lord promised Abraham that his seed would be as numerous as the sand on the seashore and the stars in the sky," Father said. "Pharaoh can't kill us off, either in the river or the mud pits, if that is what he intends. What the Lord speaks will be done, because the Lord speaks the truth. We will grow and prosper, despite what our circumstances tell us right now."

I told Father that it was horrible for the Egyptians to believe in a god that accepted human sacrifices. I decided to ask him a question that had been on my mind for a long time. "It's said that Hapi lives in a cave somewhere on the banks of Iteru. Does our God have a home somewhere?"

Av led me outside again. He placed his hands on my shoulders and turned me until we faced the southeast. "There's a sacred mountain deep within the wilderness," he told me. "Nomads say that sometimes a violent storm rages at the summit. The peak is embroiled in thick, swirling clouds. Lightning flashes from within, and thunder roars. A trumpet sounds deep inside the granite face. It's said that at this time, God inhabits this mountain. He moves from his home in heaven to the top of the mountain on earth to be closer to his people."

The stars shone like a million lanterns tonight, and I was reminded of an Egyptian painting I saw long ago and never forgot. In it the sky was painted like a sheet of water and the stars rode in boats across the vast universe.

"Father, do you think our God sees what's happening to us? Do you think he knows what the Egyptians want to do to our babies?"

Av touched my cheek with the back of his hand. "I am your father and you are my child. Do I see when a tear touches your cheek?"

"Yes, I know you do."

"Do you think I would care if someone hurt you?" he asked me tenderly.

"Oh yes, Father. I know you would."

"Well, our God cares about us in the same way. We are his children. He sees all, and he knows all. He will answer our prayers, perhaps not in the way we expect, but an answer will be delivered to us."

I believe Father, and now I have peace in my heart. I will wait for God's answer.

Morning

Miriam shared a piece of unsettling news with me. Her mother is with child. Jochebed had suspected it for several weeks, but she didn't want to say anything until she knew for sure. Obviously, it's the worst possible time to bear a child. She's beside herself with worry.

She said Amram has been praying for the past day and a half and has not emerged from his bedroom. His heart is heavy with concern for our people, and now he bears the weight of concern for his family and his unborn child.

I overheard Mother and Father again. "I'll go over and talk with her," Em announced. "If she moistens barley and wheat seeds with a few drops of her urine each day, she will know soon enough if she carries a boy or a girl."

"Then what?" Father asked her. "God forbid if the wheat sprouts and not the barley and she discovers she carries a son in her womb. She'll fret for the next nine moons. Leave well enough alone, Kezia. It will be what it will be."

I heard Em mutter a bit, as was her custom when she didn't agree with Father, but she said nothing more on the subject.

Later

Mother grabbed my hand and pulled me out the door after Av left with Becher this morning. "Come, we must go and pay a visit to Jochebed. She needs us now."

I started to say that I thought Av had told her to leave things alone, but then I remembered I wasn't supposed to have heard their conversation in the first place. We arrived to find Atera in a state of emotional distress. Her eyes were red and puffy, and her cheeks were wet with tears. Jochebed was trying to comfort her. I've never seen Becher's wife in this state. She's bright like the sun and always filled with faith and joy.

"What is it?" I asked Miriam. "What's wrong now?"

Miriam pulled me into her bedroom. "Her

daughter Eva is not only with child, but she carries a son."

My heart sank. It should be a time of rejoicing when our women carry new life in their wombs, but now it's a time of tears and sorrow. I was about to speak when Miriam touched my lips with her fingers. "My mother has news as well."

We joined the women in the next room and sat down on mats that covered the dirt floor. Jochebed leaned close. "You are my dearest friends, and I trust you with my life. What I'm about to tell you, you must not tell anyone else. Amram has left to talk with Izri [that's Father's name] at the market."

"Of course, of course," Em reassured her. "Your words will stay in our hearts but will never leave this room. Don't worry. It's done."

Jochebed sighed, and a small smile lifted the corners of her lips. "When Amram discovered that I was with child, he began to pray and pray. As you know, he's an honorable man and God's favor shines on him. He awakened me in the still of the night and shared something, which I will share with you now. The Lord told him that the child I carry in my womb is the one the scribe spoke of to Pharaoh."

Mother's eyes widened. Her mouth moved, but it was a moment before her voice followed. "You mean you'll give birth to a boy?" she asked.

"Yes, Kezia."

Em nodded, and the room was silent for a moment. I looked at Miriam, and she nodded as well.

"You mean this innocent will be our deliverer? The one who will save us from the bondage of the Egyptians?" Atera asked.

"Yes."

The room was silent again, and I watched Mother's eyes dart back and forth with her thoughts. "How, Jochebed?" she asked. "I believe what you say, but how will all of this happen? It seems impossible. We've been fortunate so far. The Egyptians haven't found our baby boys, but how long can this last? What will you do when your boy is born? How long can you keep him hidden?"

Em is given to worry, and Jochebed knows this.

She placed her hands over Mother's and stroked them. Then she pulled Atera's clenched fingers apart and held them in her own. "We don't have any answers, but our God does. Atera, your grandson won't be born for many moons, nor will my son.

"In the meantime, we must do what we can to help the sons who are born to us today and tomorrow and the next day. We'll be forced to operate in secret, and we must be careful that no one finds out. Innocent lives will be put in jeopardy if we're exposed."

So much has happened in recent weeks, too much for any of us to grasp. Eva and Jochebed carry sons, and my very own Miriam will be sister to the one God chose to deliver us from our bondage. If this baby is the answer to our prayers, then Father was right. God doesn't always answer our prayers in a way we expect.

Later ~A Secret Mission

Em pulled me aside and emphasized what Jochebed had told us at Miriam's house earlier. We must do whatever is necessary to help the families in their time of need. She said I could help her prepare batches of honey, juice from the silphium plant, and powder from a mineral called natron to make a natural concoction that prevents fertile women from becoming pregnant.

I found this idea troublesome and told Mother so, but I didn't tell her that Father's words were going round and round in my head—*"Leave well enough alone, Kezia. It will be what it will be."*

"Laila!" she scolded. "Do you want our women to give birth to sons who may well be murdered?"

I was aghast. "Of course not, Em."

"Well then, you agree that it isn't fair that innocents are slaughtered because they're boys. Let the women wait until the crisis passes. If their wombs are fertile now, they will be fertile again. It's only for a season. It will serve you well to learn this lesson sooner rather than later.

"Be prepared," she warned me. "Egyptians will rove among us now, spying on those who are with child, waiting for them to give birth. We must get word out that all pregnant women must hide their pregnancies. When their bellies grow so round that they can't hide their condition, they must stay in their homes. We'll bring food to them or arrange for other women who can. All baby boys will be hidden at birth and can't be taken outside. If there is danger, the mothers must get word out to us. The babies will be taken to a safe house until the danger passes."

I feel proud that Em considers me old enough and mature enough to be included in this important mission. I just wish it were a happier one. When I put down my pen, I'll pray for the Lord to help us. Av has always said that if we don't know a direction in life, we should pray and ask God to show us. He sees all, and he knows all. He's the best one to guide us. Yes! That will be my prayer—for the Lord to guide us in our mission.

A Funeral Procession at Dusk

Miriam and I walked to the river to draw water. It has become a ritual of ours in recent days. We use the time to discuss the news without fear that someone will overhear our words. The trail we take to the river is usually empty, but if someone crosses our path, we change our conversation in a casual way. Mother has stressed that we can't be too careful now.

The water was just a stone's throw away when the haunting wail of the mourners met our ears. It sent a chill through me, and Miriam clutched my hand. Since we live on the edge of Goshen, we're often witness to Egyptian funeral processions. I've never liked them, and today was no exception. We scrambled backward and crouched behind a tall, leafy bush.

A priest in a long white robe led the procession. In one hand he waved a golden pot-like vessel—a censer, it's called—with holes on its top for burning incense to waft through. With the other hand he sprinkled milk on the path in front of him. The coffin rested on top of a boat-shaped frame that was covered with a canopy and set on a cart pulled by several oxen. A widow and two women mourners sat beside the mummy.

I watched a similar procession once when I was with Em. She told me that the two women mourners represented the goddesses Isis and Nepthys. The Egyptians believe that the winged goddesses are protectors of the dead. Isis is thought to represent the wind. Her voice wails and moans as she glides through the trees. She sits at the foot of every coffin, and her sister Nepthys sits at the head. They spread their wings to protect the body within.

The important guests walked behind the cart followed by several dozen mourners dressed in blue. They tore at their clothes and hair as they wailed and screamed. Their faces were contorted in grief.

"It must be a royal subject who died," Miriam whispered. "There are so many mourners."

Miriam is right. Professional mourners are hired by families to express their grief. The richer the family, the more mourners they can afford to pay.

The servants trailed the procession. They carried the goods and the furniture that would be placed in the tomb with the mummy. There would be food and wine so the mummy would not be hungry, clothing and blankets to keep him warm, writing supplies and perhaps a chess board to wile away his time, wigs and eye paint so he can beautify himself, and even a harpoon so he might hunt or defend himself.

There would be everything an Egyptian believed he would need in the afterlife. There would even be tiny clay replicas of boats to carry the dead on their journey to their new life.

The tombs are located on the west bank of Iteru, where the Egyptians believe life ends with the setting of the sun. Since everyone lives on the east bank, where life begins with the rising of the sun, all funeral processions have to cross the river.

To the Egyptians, dying means coming to land on the other side. The passage into the next world is called a crossing.

Miriam and I watched as the coffin was transported into a large cedar funerary boat. The boat swayed in the water as the family and the mourners climbed aboard. The furniture and all of the goods were lifted up last. The boat was pushed away from the shore with large oars to begin its crossing to the other side.

We held each other's hands for comfort and walked home, our water jugs swaying empty at our sides. I have begun to wonder in recent weeks how it is that our people came to live in a land like Egypt. The Egyptians' beliefs are so different from our own. I also wonder how it is that I didn't pay much attention to these differences until now.

Many Weeks Pass ~ First Star of Morning

I slept lightly last night and was easily awakened by Av's footsteps across the dirt floor. I heard our door open and close, and I wrapped my tunic around my shoulders and followed him outside. The sky was still dark, though a sliver of light painted the horizon.

"Do you see it, Father?" I asked.

"Not yet, Laila, but any day now," he told me. He wasn't surprised to see me; I've joined him every morning for the last week. Egypt anxiously awaits the rising of the star Sirius. Each year it fades from view for several moons. When it alights in the sky again, the flood follows within days. Soon we'll rise to find it glowing in the infant sky just before sunrise.

There's a crackle of anticipation in the air. No one knows what the river will bring as it rushes towards its demise in the Great Sea. If Iteru floods too much, there is destruction and the land weeps. If it floods too little, there could be famine. The Egyptians offer many prayers to Hapi in the hope that he will shine his favor upon them and bring a bountiful flood year. It's common now to hear the women and children sing words like these on the riverbanks: *"Come and prosper! Come and prosper! O Iteru, come and prosper! O you who make men to live through his flocks and his flocks through his orchards! Come and prosper, come, O Iteru, come and prosper!"*

Father pointed toward a flickering light far

above the dawn in the eastern sky. It was the first star of morning. "If we were Egyptians, we would say that this star has just returned from his stay in the underworld."

It seems sad that something as beautiful and full of promise as the first star of morning has been to a place as dark as the underworld. I prefer to think of the stars as blinking beacons sent by God to light our way and give us hope.

Roving Egyptians

Mother was right when she said there would be Egyptians roving among us now. It's clear to everyone that they're watching us.

A short while ago, just after lunch, a man knocked on our door and asked to see Av about a seal. He knocked in a peculiar series of raps that sounded almost musical. Mother heard and told me to open the door at once. I led him into the workroom while she waited in the next room, wringing her hands. Father and the stranger spoke in hushed voices, and after a few minutes the man left. Av came out and handed Mother a shard of pottery. "Pelet brought this," he told her.

I peered over her shoulder and saw an address written in tiny characters. Mother read it, then took it into Father's workroom and did the unexpected. She laid it on the worktable, covered it with a cloth, and smashed it with a heavy stone hammerhead. When she lifted the cloth, clay crumbs and brown dust were scattered on the table.

Em turned toward me. "Do you remember the secret mission that helps the mothers and babies?"

I told her I did.

"Well, the man who came here is one of our messengers. His name is Pelet. He inquired about a seal in case he was followed. The real reason for his visit was to deliver the address written on the shard. It belongs to a woman named Helsa who is about to give birth. She believes she carries a son."

Father spoke in a low voice. "Go to her. Atera and Jochebed are already there. You must be careful and act as normal as possible; the house is watched. I have an idea, and if it works, you can take Helsa to the safe house to give birth. They will hide her and her baby there for a time."

"And if it doesn't work?" Em asked him. The room grew still. Even the magpies had stopped their twittering in the trees outside.

"I don't know," he answered. "We must take the first step of faith. It's the most important one. Thereafter, we must trust in the Lord to direct our footsteps, one footstep at a time."

Mother leaves at dusk. Needless to say, I'm not allowed to go this time because she thinks it's too dangerous. I'll wait until she leaves, and then I'll go to Miriam. There must be a way we can help.

That Night

I'm sitting in a cramped cellar with Miriam. A burning wick floats in a pool of olive oil in a clay lamp beside me. It's our only light. The heavy footsteps of a man traipse across the floor, but it's my ceiling he walks upon. The earth around me thunders with the vibrations. They stop. Two lighter pairs of footsteps belong to women padding in different directions in their bare feet.

I'm thankful to Miriam, who made me go back for my diary. She reminded me again of my writing gift and the importance of recording the events of the days at hand. It's a time of great change for our people; she was right about that. This evening proved that. I should go back to where I left off . . .

Becher arrived at the same time Em opened the door to leave. Mother was late, and the shadows of night had already descended upon Goshen. She parted her lips to scream, but Becher was quick, and he covered her mouth with his hand. "No, Kezia, it's me, your hobble-legged friend."

She slumped into his arms. "You startled me, you old fool." She was annoyed with him, but her words were laced with affection.

"Come inside before you leave," he whispered to her. "I have something to tell you." Hoshaiah followed him inside, and I heard Mother sigh, but she didn't say a word.

The door was shut before Becher spoke. "Take the alley north two streets past Helsa's house. Go west, and approach the house from behind. There's a narrow window there, but it's wide enough for you to climb through. They're watching for you."

She left, and I told Av that I needed to see Miriam, which was true. "Take a lamp with you, Laila," he called from the back room. "The moon is dim tonight."

I picked up the clay bowl Em had lit and left on the small table in the hall. I knew she walked to Helsa's house without one so that she wouldn't draw attention to herself. I carried the lamp toward Miriam's house and was grateful I had it. The moon was just a thin slice in the sky, and the houses were dark. Though our days begin and end with the sun, lamps burn in our homes until well into the night. On this evening, we saw the glow of no lamps in the windows.

I reached Miriam's house just as a lick of wind snuffed out the flame. A wisp of smoke blew into the air. As soon as I reached her door, it opened and she pulled me inside.

"What can we do?" I asked her.

"We can go to Helsa's house," she announced.

Her quick reply told me she'd already come up with a plan. I wasn't surprised. Miriam is a born leader. I'm a good worker, and I can follow direction well, but I don't have the quick, bold leadership qualities Miriam possesses.

"Don't ask me what we'll do once we get there," she said. "I've just felt for the past hour that we should go. Our mothers will be too busy with Helsa to be angry with us."

We took the lamp with us in case we needed it later, but we didn't light it. I led Miriam north through the alley, the same way Becher had directed Em.

"Why are all the houses so dark?" I whispered. "It's scary. I've never seen Goshen like this."

"The people know they're being watched, so they snuff out the lamps at nights to make it hard for the Egyptians to see into their homes," she whispered back.

Just as we reached the end of the alley, we spotted a tall, dark shadow of a man one block west. He paced back and forth. A long, pleated skirt fell to his sandaled feet and was knotted at his hips with a fringed sash. A short, wide cape hung from his shoulders, and even the darkness of the night couldn't hide the sword that hung from a sheath at his side. It was obvious by his dress that he was in service of the king.

Miriam pulled me back, and we crouched out of sight beside the wall of one of the houses. "It's an Egyptian," she said with a shudder. "We can't get past him, but that's not the worst part. Our mothers can't get Helsa to the safe house without being seen. They won't even know he's there until they've climbed out the window and it's too late."

We sat for several moments in silence. The night seemed surreal to me then, and it seems surreal to me now as I recount the events from the secret cellar.

"Miriam." I squeezed her arm. "Father told Mother this just before she left. He said, 'We must take the first step of faith. It's the most important one. Thereafter, we must trust in the Lord to direct our footsteps, one footstep at a time.'"

The eerie silence of the night was interrupted by dark, guttural voices in the Egyptian tongue. They spoke too fast for me to understand. We peered around the corner. A slighter Egyptian had joined the first. The newcomer was facing south, *away* from Helsa's house, and the other didn't like it. Their voices grew louder, and I watched the first one grip the handle of his sword. The other patted him on the back in a conciliatory fashion and coaxed him away.

"Now!" Miriam cried. "Your father was right. God has given us our next footstep. Let's go. We can warn the others." We walked by the spot where the men had stood, but there was no sign of them anywhere.

Helsa's house was one story, and it was dark and quiet like the others. A face appeared in the narrow window in the back of the house as we approached it. It was Atera. Her eyes were wide in disbelief, but she said nothing. She held out her hand and helped us through the window. Mother and Jochebed ran into the room, and Helsa peered from the doorway. They didn't have a chance to speak.

"You must leave now," Miriam whispered. "There was one Egyptian man watching the house when we reached the end of the alley. Then another came and argued with him, and they went away. It's safe now, but who knows when they'll return."

Helsa was holding her huge belly. Her husband appeared and stood beside her. "Yes," he said. "I agree. We'll take our chances and leave for the safe house now. The Lord has delivered the answer to our prayers through these brave young women."

I'll continue my story later. The thump on the door above my head means Helsa is about to deliver her baby. She must come below into the cellar, where there's light and where she and the baby can't be heard. The door is hidden in the floor beneath a rug. It can be pulled open from above, but it can only be latched and unlatched from below. Miriam and I will wait in the darkened rooms above with Em and the others.

The Morning Watch

It's three hours past sunup, and I awakened just a short while ago. It was a late night for all of us, but especially for Av and Em. I heard the soft lull of their voices as I drifted into my dreams. I'll continue where I left off last evening . . .

The safe house was farther away than I thought it would be, but thanks to the Lord it was an uneventful walk. There were no signs of any Egyptians until we reached the house and Shiphrah and Puah greeted us at the door. We hadn't seen them since the last meeting at Amram and Jochebed's home.

They pulled us in and bolted the door. By this time Helsa was whimpering, and Shiphrah led her up the stairs to a storage room in the back of the house. There were no windows in this room, so a lamp could be lit as long as the door was closed.

Puah walked into the room, carrying a plaster of sea salt, wheat, and rushes from the river. She placed these on Helsa's abdomen to help induce delivery. Miriam and I were given permission to go below into the cellar, where we could take our lamp and write or talk freely. As we descended the stairs, the midwives were chanting, "Make the heart of the deliverer strong, and keep alive the one that is coming."

Two hours later I heard the thump on the floor above my head. We unlatched the door and climbed out. Helsa was lowered into the cellar and Shiphrah and Puah carried the birth stool below. The door was closed, and we heard the bolt slide into place as Atera smoothed the rug. We waited in the shadowy house, and in less than one hour, we heard the muffled cries of a baby.

Mother said later that it was a bittersweet moment for the mother and the father, and she's right, of course. It was sweet because it was the birth of their first child and because Helsa bore her husband a prized, healthy son. It was also bitter because Helsa bore her husband a prized, healthy son. He was called Aziel, which means "God is might."

Father, Becher, and Amram were relieved when we returned. They suspected that Miriam and I had gone to Helsa's house, and they'd spent the evening in prayer. When we told them the story of the Egyptian spy and the man who had argued with him and led him away, Av said a miracle had taken place.

He told us about an Egyptian customer who worked in the government who had been a loyal friend for many years. He'd tried to contact him through secret channels to ask for his help, but he couldn't reach him.

"Then who was the Egyptian man who led the other away?" I asked Av.

"Once again, I have no answers for you," he replied. There was a soft light in his eyes. "Perhaps it was my friend after all, although I don't know how it could have been. Perhaps it was an angel of the Lord sent to us in our time of need. All we need to know is that our God intervened on our behalf. That we know for sure."

Amram directed his attention to Miriam and me. "What you did was dangerous; however, I can't admonish you. I believe the Lord used you tonight. He placed you at the end of the alley to witness the miracle and to let the women know it was time to move to the safe house. We don't know if the first Egyptian came back later to watch the house for a time. I laud you for your bravery and for your service."

I do feel proud, as does Miriam, but there's no time to dwell on it. Now we must believe God for more miracles. Jochebed will no longer be able to hide her pregnancy. Her belly grows too round to disguise her condition, and she'll be forced to stay inside during the day. It must be the same way with Atera and Becher's daughter, Eva.

My faith is renewed on this blessed day, however. All of us, mother, Atera, and Jochebed included, took the first, most important step of faith. I believe that the Lord guided our footsteps, one footstep at a time, just like Av said he would.

To the Market

I strolled with Av to the market at the quay, or river landing, today. It's the last time we'll come before the flood. Golden mimosa and poinciana trees, aflame with their yellow and red blossoms, line the river by the landing places. Dirty sailors who haven't bathed in many days unload exotic, priceless freight. When I come with Father, he allows me to wander up and down the quay.

I inherited from him a fascination for the Phoenician merchant ships. He says the Phoenicians are the greatest sailors of all time and their ships are the most advanced. They are not only coastal sailors, sailing by day from village to village, using landmarks to help them navigate, but also brave sailors of the deep water. The Phoenicians travel farther in their sophisticated ships than most men dare to sail in their dreams. At night they're guided by the heavens, the Phoenician Star in particular.

One of these ships pulled up to the dock as I stepped onto the waterside platform. Its planks gleamed with the finest wood cut from the cedars of Lebanon. A square red-and-white-striped sail hung from the tall mast. A large, round vase of burnt clay, with two handles at the top, was filled with drinkable water and was rigged upright to the stern.

Several sailors stood on the side of the great ship and handed crates of wine and oils to the sailors on the dock. Long planks of wrapped cedar wood used for ships, coffins, and fine furniture were also unloaded.

Ships from Nubia, to the south, unloaded gold, though it wasn't for the purpose of trade. Pharaoh demands that the Nubians pay tribute in gold as a means to show their submission to Egypt. The ships from Punt carried incense as well as tall, green incense-bearing trees like the olibanum, whose dried gum is frankincense. These trees were bound for the king and would be planted in the temple gardens, still fresh and fragrant.

Trade ships from Syro-Palestine carried medicines such as healing ointments. They often bring oils and horses too, and I've even seen chariots unloaded. I'm disappointed that I didn't see horses on this day, but my patience was rewarded when screaming monkeys were lifted to the docks in wooden cages. Cattle were herded off as well, but they're not as exciting. I can go into the fields and see cattle any day.

There were piles of spotted leopard skins, used by the Egyptian priests, and other odd things: giraffe tails, ostrich feathers, elephant tusks sewn up in hides, eggs, and beautiful painted pottery from Crete.

At the close of the day, these same ships would return to their homes heavy with Egyptian merchandise like gold, fine metalwork, papyrus plants, papyrus paper, and high quality linen made from the flax plant, which grows in abundance here.

By the time I wandered into the marketplace, Father was ready to leave and so was I. The din overwhelms me. Men and women haggle over prices, ready to barter grain and oil for fruits and vegetables, honey, or some of the more exotic fare. Merchants squat in their stalls with their wares spread around them in baskets.

I helped Av carry our baskets loaded with food. I feel content and tired in a good way, like I've seen a bit of the world but have come home again.

Sirius Rises!

I had just slipped my feet into my sandals when Av called to me. "Laila! Come quickly!" I let the other sandal drop from my hand, and I flew outside with one foot bare.

We stood as we had every morning for several weeks. At first glance, the heavens looked the same. The west was fading into blue, but the tip of the horizon to the east was brushed with red and orange. The sky was still dark enough to shimmer with stars, and then I saw it! It was a clear constellation of a dog.

"There we have it," Father murmured. "The constellation represents the going up of the goddess Sothis." He pulled me close to him and held up his arm and pointed. "There, at the tip of the dog's nose, is the brightest jewel of all. It's Sirius, the one all eyes in Egypt have waited for."

We've entered the Egyptian new year and the flood season called Akhet. Any day now the great river Iteru will flood its banks.

Several Days Later ~ The Start of the Flood

Miriam and I went to the river this afternoon to fill our jugs, but we withdrew before we neared the banks. We were close enough to see that the water was colored a turbid red. We ran back—Miriam to her house and I to mine.

"The flood has begun! The flood has begun!" I cried as I ran through the door. Av and Becher stood at the doorway to the workshop, and Em stood at the top of the stairs.

The two men looked at one another and nodded. Mother had tears in her eyes. In my excitement I'd forgotten that when the river floods, the men are called up by Pharaoh to build the store cities. Em and I will be left alone for about three moons, as will Atera and Jochebed and most of the other women in Goshen.

My heart is heavy as I write this. Our beloved men will leave in a day or two.

Two Days Later

Father left at sunup with Amram and Becher. He hugged Mother and me tight and promised to return in a few moons. Then he was gone. It's a day's walk to the store cities, so when the sun sets this evening, we know they'll have arrived.

Em is cleaning the house now, trying to stay busy. Miriam came by earlier. She made me promise to come to her house and play some games with her. She doesn't like to leave her mother for long now, and I don't blame her.

I took the broom from Em's hand a short while ago and offered to sweep the downstairs while she rested for a bit. She hadn't stopped sweeping since Av left four hours before. As I swept, I worked up the courage to ask her something I'd never wanted to know before.

"Mother?" She was sitting on the clay dais that runs along the length of the wall, and I think she was daydreaming. My words interrupted her, and she lifted her eyes to mine.

"Is it true that Father will be forced to work in the mud pits?" I paused and rested my hands on the top of the broom handle. I didn't look at her while I waited for her answer. I was afraid of what she would say.

Em was quiet for a long time. "Yes, Laila." She sighed. "I believe so, although your father has never spoken of it. He doesn't want to worry me, but that's what I've heard as well. They'll put him to work engraving the pillars and the stones first, but, yes, it's likely he'll work in the mud pits, making the bricks.

"Laila, your father is a man of honor. He wouldn't want special treatment because he's a craftsman. If men are sweating in the mud and the straw, he would want to share their burden, and he would want us to respect his decision."

I wondered about Becher and how he would work in the mud pits with only one good leg, but I didn't ask. I'll save that question for another day. I'll write more when I return from Miriam's house. I told her I would bring my Dogs and Jackals game. I wish I could remember where I put it.

Evening ~ Dogs and Jackals

I found my game. Em said she'd seen it in Father's workshop, and she was right. When I walked in, I spotted it right away on his table, tucked into a dusty corner. I remembered then that we'd played it together one day when I was bored. I picked up the board and smiled at the memory. He's been gone for less than a day, and I'm teary eyed every time I think of him. What will it be like for me in the coming weeks?

Mother decided to get out of the house and come with me. We stopped by Atera's, and she joined us as well. She walked out of the door and whistled, and Em looked at me and shrugged her shoulders. Then we saw the reason for our neighbor's odd behavior: Hoshaiah sauntered out the door behind her.

Atera smiled when she saw our faces. I was grateful that some of the light had returned to her eyes. "I'm his surrogate parent when Becher is away. What can I do?" she said and threw up her hands.

The visit was good for all of us. The three women sat and gossiped as usual, and Miriam and I played Dogs and Jackals for hours. Father made my board many years ago, and he did a fine job with it. It's a rectangular wooden box, and it stands on four animal legs. A palm tree is painted in the middle, and there are fifty-eight holes that run up and down either side of the trunk and along all of the sides of the box.

I've admired Dogs and Jackals game boards at the market. The boards there are made of ivory, and the game pieces are carved from ebony. Father said one day I would own one like that. I laugh when I think of his words. A board as beautiful as that belongs in the pharaoh's palace or at least in his tomb!

The game pieces are stored in the drawer within the box. There are ten short sticks. Five are carved with the head of a dog and the other five with the head of a jackal. The first player to put all five of his pawns into the five holes near the top of the tree wins.

Miriam and I took turns allowing Aaron to put the pieces into the peg holes. It was easier this way. If we didn't, he would have grabbed the pieces and run away, and we would have spent the whole day chasing after him.

The women were so engaged in their conversation, we decided to take out Miriam's game of Senet. We aren't allowed to play it very often. It's an Egyptian game that represents the soul's journey into the underworld. If a player is very good at the game, it is believed he will have success on his soul's final journey. I can understand why our mothers aren't fond of the game, but to us it's just a fun diversion, and a silly one at that.

This game is also made from a rectangular box, but the board on top is painted with thirty squares in three even rows of ten. The pieces are cones, triangles, and reels, and we throw sticks to determine the number of spaces we can move.

If three sticks point upward, then we're allowed to move three spaces, and so on.

I won both games of Dogs and Jackals, and Miriam won the game of Senet. In this way, the evening passed quickly and our thoughts didn't dwell on the loved ones we missed.

A Sad Reminder

Atera brought disturbing news to the house today. "Another infant has been drowned," she told us. "The mother lived near Helsa, and in the middle of the night, all of the neighbors were awakened by a great commotion. There were angry shouts and the screams of a woman and the cry of a baby."

Atera was wringing her hands. "Apparently, an Egyptian came into the house and pulled the boy from his mother's arms. That was three days ago."

Mother gasped. "That makes three drownings we've heard of just this week. Have they found the safe houses yet? Have you heard about Helsa and the baby?"

"No, no," Atera answered. "Helsa is still at the safe house, and they haven't discovered it yet. Nor have they found the other ones."

"Does Jochebed know any of this?" Em asked.

"I don't think so, Kezia, but I can't be sure. I don't know what others tell her."

It's another somber reminder that our world isn't safe. Em said our people used to worry that our women and children would be lost in childbirth or succumb to illness. We used to fear that our men would die at the hands of marauders. Now our greatest threat comes from our neighbors, who once welcomed us into their land.

"This is no longer our home," Mother said. Her voice was heavy and filled with sorrow. "It's clear that we're no longer welcome here."

Egypt Is Flooded

The land is now covered in a sheet of brown water. Villages protrude like islands. Palm trees, which once stood tall and proud on the riverbanks, huddle together like warriors. Water climbs their trunks the way naked children used to.

The flood season is a time of great celebration though, and Miriam and I venture outside every day to watch the activity. We're never disappointed. Boats, which navigate the swollen waterway with ease, surge upon the river. Many of them are festooned with garlands of ribbons, flowers, and leaves. The garlands drape the boat end to end.

Yesterday we were fortunate to see the procession of a sacred festival. A statue of a god, dressed in colorful linen and jewelry of gold, silver, and deep blue (which could only be lapis lazuli), was encased in a shrine and set on top of a ceremonial barque. A barque is a sailing ship with three masts, and this one was carried to the river on the shoulders of the priests. A long parade followed: soldiers, singers, drummers, acrobatic dancers, and musicians. Dignitaries and even the king's chariots were part of the grand procession.

They crossed the river where booths filled with refreshments and offerings to the gods were lined up from the edge of Iteru to the temples. The air was smoky with incense, and we listened to the jangle of the sistrum. It's a rattle instrument that's said to mimic the music of the breeze when it shakes the papyrus reeds. This sound is said to soothe the gods and goddesses.

Hymns like this one have been sung by the Egyptians since the start of the flood: *"Hail to you Hapi, Sprung from earth, Come to nourish Egypt . . . Food provider, bounty maker, Who creates all that is good! . . . Conqueror of the Two Lands, He fills the stores, Makes bulge the barns, Gives bounty to the poor."*

Mother says this year looks to be one of the best flood years yet. There isn't so much water that our homes are washed away, but there's enough to leave a thick layer of silt when the river recedes. This year, she says, we'll have an excellent harvest.

For all of this the Egyptians give thanks to Hapi. Our people give thanks to the Lord.

Diary Two
Several Moons Later
1526 BC

The End of Akhet

It's hard to believe that three moons have passed since I last wrote, but little has taken place. When the flood season is upon us, the days linger.

Last night our good friends Shiphrah and Puah surprised us. They knocked at our door and slipped in quickly when Em answered. Tomorrow, they told us, we must invite Jochebed and Miriam, Atera, Bernice and her new daughter, and many more friends. They said they would prepare an Egyptian feast for us before the passing of Akhet.

True to their word, they returned in the morning with their long arms laden with baskets of food. They settled themselves in the kitchen for the better part of the afternoon. I was put in charge of the *ful medames*, a simple fava bean stew. With their guidance, I boiled the fava beans until they were tender, drained them, added crushed cloves of garlic, and mashed everything up. This was served with eggs.

They made hummus by cooking and mashing chickpeas. They added the juice of a lemon, crushed garlic, and olive oil. It was a creamy paste, which we spread on our bread. To these dishes we added roasted duck and dried fish. Shiphrah prepared sweet wine cakes. In a large clay bowl, she mixed flour, wine, cumin, anise seed, chopped cheese, animal fat, and a beaten egg. She shaped the dough into twelve small cakes, placed each on an edible leaf, and baked them.

At the end of the afternoon, just before the guests arrived, Puah made tiger nut sweets, my favorite! She blended fresh dates with a bit of water, then added cinnamon and chopped walnuts. After shaping them into balls, she rolled them in honey and chopped almonds. These sweets are similar to the fig cakes Em prepares. The difference is that Mother prepares them with sycamore figs instead of dates. Either way, they're delicious.

It was a glorious celebration spent in the company of our good friends, but now I have a confession to make. I'm anxious for the flood season to be over and for Av and the rest of our men to return to us. I long for life to settle into a normal, predictable routine again.

Em said it was good to see Jochebed out of her house, but she's worried about her. Her belly is very large, and she's not due to give birth for several more moons. I asked her what this meant, and she told me that perhaps Jochebed is further along than she realizes. If this is the case, she'll give birth much sooner than we thought.

Flies and Vermin

We are plagued. Every flood season, the moist air is thick with flies, gnats, and mosquitoes. They lay thousands of eggs in the pools of water left by the receding river and in the full canals that cross the land. Vermin swarm through the moist fields and crawl through the villages. They slink into our homes and burrow holes into our sacks of grain.

I watched Mother smear fat across our threshold and along the base of our house. "Come on," she called to me. "You can help too. This isn't an easy job without your father here."

I hesitated before I dipped my fingers into the white grease. It was thick and slippery. "Where did you get this?" I asked her.

"Never mind," she said crossly. "All you need to know is that it keeps the rats away."

We went around the whole house and even spread some beneath the lower windows and on the grain sacks. When we were through, Em handed the bowl to me. "Now go and see if Jochebed needs any. If she does, you and Miriam take care of it for her."

When I got to Jochebed's house, Miriam took one look at the fat and squished up her nose. "Do you know what this is?"

"No, do you?"

"I'll tell you after we spread it around," she replied. "There were two rats in the kitchen this morning."

We emptied the bowl and washed our hands before Miriam would tell me.

"Don't get upset," she said. Her voice was soft and soothing. "Remember, your mother got it from the Egyptians. It's an effective way to keep away the vermin."

I was suspicious. "I don't think I want to know anymore."

"Well, you have to," she replied. "It's cat fat."

"Cat fat?" I cried. "*Cat* fat?"

Miriam told me not to think about it, and I'm trying not to. At least I can understand why the rats stay away. Mother said that if the problem persists, we'll have to get our own cat and not just fat from someone else's. I'm trying not to think about that either. I've seen them at the marketplace penned up in small cages. They snarl and hiss and claw at anyone who comes near. I wonder if they know about the fat.

Twilight

I'm sitting on my mat beneath the mosquito netting Em and I tacked up. It wasn't easy. Three long beams run along the length of the ceiling, and we had to stand on our tiptoes on a chair to attach the netting with nails. We did the same in the other bedroom where Mother sleeps.

I'm covered with mosquito bites and red welts, which are the result of fly stings. Em applied fresh *ben* oil to take away the sting and the itch. Tomorrow we'll try a different tactic—palm wine. If we apply it all over our skin, it should discourage the insects from biting. The past few nights I was awakened by mosquitoes buzzing in my ear. Now that I'm safe beneath the netting, I'll sleep like a lamb.

I was about to leave Miriam's house earlier today when Jochebed called me over to her. She took my hand and placed it on the underside of her growing belly. I felt a ripple and then a strong jab, and I jumped a little in surprise. Miriam laughed.

"The baby is kicking," Jochebed told me. "It's a good sign. It means he's strong and healthy. Tell your mother that he's dropped into place. It won't be long now."

When Em came in to kiss me good night, I told her what Jochebed had said. She nodded and smiled. I believe her exact words were "That child is called of the Lord, Laila. He'll emerge from the womb when his heavenly Father tells him it's time."

Morning

I heard a sweet sound earlier that I haven't heard for several weeks. Miriam was singing as she skipped toward our house. Her voice was so joyful, I thought she must have wonderful news, and I dashed outside to meet her. "Oh, Laila!" she cried and hugged me tight. "There's word that our fathers will be home in a day or two!"

Mother said she could be right. The flood is over, and the planting season is upon us. The men must return home to plant their crops in time for the harvest.

I've spent the last few hours in Av's workshop with a broom, a cleaning cloth, and a bit of oil. I began on one side of his long workbench, wiping away the brown dirt that had settled upon it like a soft coverlet. I picked up his stylus and each of his chisels, files, hammerheads, and gouges, and I rubbed them clean. The metal shavings, the clay crumbs, and the stone bits were swept into a neat pile at the back of the room, when a red stone caught my eye.

My fingers sifted gently through the debris, and I lifted the stone from the pile and wiped it with the corner of my cloth. I knew it was a ruby, but I was surprised by its deep, flaming color. Father had taught me that the intensity of the color is a good indication of a stone's worth. My finger caressed the surface and found several small chips, which rendered it worthless to a buyer. I found it exquisite and tucked it into the pocket of my tunic.

Av allowed me to sift through the piles so I could pick out the gems and stones before he threw them away. These were the odd bits he couldn't use; they were either too small, or they were of poor quality, or they were chipped or scratched. To me, they're priceless treasures. I keep them in a basket tucked into a wall hollow in my bedroom, covered with a soft cloth. There are thick slivers of turquoise and lapis lazuli, small chunks of pink ruby, slices of white and translucent alabaster, scraps of silver, and even a piece of gold hidden at the very bottom.

One day Father will polish them for me, and I will make a necklace. For now, I like them in my basket or spread out in front of me where they shine in the sunlight that streams through my window.

I was through, but I stopped to admire my handiwork from the doorway before I left. I had even oiled the wooden stools, and they gleamed like new wood. Av will be pleased.

Evening ~ A Miracle in the Cellar

Oh, much has happened! Where do I begin? Miriam reminded me again, "Write! Write! Don't leave out a word!"

The sun had set, and I walked into my bedroom, carrying the lamp Em had lit for me. I pulled back my netting, when I heard a whisper at the window. I was so startled, I dropped the lamp. The oil spilled, the flame was extinguished, and I was left in the dark, frozen in fear.

I listened again for the whisper. There was no sound. Instead, I saw something fly into the room and land at my feet. Miriam's silver bracelet shone in the moonlight! I went to the high window, stood on my tiptoes, and peered down. Miriam was staring up at me. "Thank goodness," she whispered. "Laila, you must come quickly! Mother is in labor, and Atera said we don't have time to move her to the safe house. Please, hurry."

Within minutes, Em and I were walking in the shadows. We didn't dare go through the front door but snuck around the back and waited at the rear window, just as we'd done at Helsa's house. Miriam's face appeared before long, and she held out her hand. Em squeezed through first, and I followed her. If it weren't for the moonlight, there would have been no light at all. Lamps were out of the question again.

"Mother and Atera are in the cellar," Miriam

said. Her voice trembled. "It's too late. When I returned, she'd already given birth."

Em gasped. "No! You said she had just gone into labor."

Miriam started to cry. "She had. I went and got Atera and then ran to get you. I wasn't gone for more than an hour."

Mother raced past her, and we followed. She pulled back the rug and tapped on the wooden door. When it opened, she peered inside the lit cellar. There were whispers, and then tears dropped from her eyes. "I thought something had happened," she said in a choked voice. "Miriam began to cry, so I assumed the worst."

I knelt down beside Em. Jochebed was sitting on a mat with blankets propped up behind her back. Her smile was tender. "You worry too much, Kezia. You always have." The baby was nestled in her arms, already nursing. "His name is Chaver. Amram insisted that we name him before he left. Somehow he knew."

Atera was crouched beside her. "The baby flew out of the birth canal. I've never seen anything like it, Kezia. I thought I wouldn't have time to get her into the cellar, but it wouldn't have mattered anyway. She didn't scream or even whimper, and neither did the baby."

Mother stood up and looked around as if she'd just remembered something. "Aaron! Where's Aaron?"

"Stop worrying," Jochebed told her. "He's asleep. He's been asleep the whole time."

Miriam was still overcome with emotion, so I sat close to her and put my arm around her shoulders. "Laila," she cried, "the Lord answered my prayers. I was so afraid when I realized we couldn't get Mother to the safe house. I asked him to please keep them quiet so no one would hear."

We stayed for several hours, but Miriam and I fell asleep on the rug beside the cellar door. I found out later that Mother cut the umbilical cord and still the baby didn't cry. She helped Atera bathe Chaver in water, and they rubbed him with salt to prevent infection. He was swaddled in long linen strips Jochebed had tucked away for him.

At Atera's insistence, we left Jochebed and Chaver in her care and walked home. There's so much more to tell, but I'm afraid this is where I must break and continue tomorrow. My eyes can't focus on one more word . . .

Early the Next Day

I would like to say that Em and I saw no shadowy figures lurking in the night as we walked home, but it wouldn't be true. We left Miriam's house and walked the same path we'd taken earlier. My mind was filled with thoughts of the new baby, Chaver, when Mother grabbed my arm and pulled me down. We crouched behind a bush, her nails digging into the skin of my arm.

I heard them before I saw them. Soft, gentle voices and the familiar creak of a crutch. As they drew near, I recognized Becher's hobbled gait and Amram's confident stride, though they both walked more slowly on this night. I flew from the bush without thinking, and they jumped a little and then froze in their tracks. Perhaps it was the just the moonlight, but their faces were without color, and their eyes were wide and bewildered.

I heard Mother beside me, and we all stared at one another before Amram found his voice. "Kezia! Laila! What on earth are you doing there in the bushes?"

There was a rumble in Becher's throat, which always preceded his laughter, and I ran into his arms. He was much thinner than I remembered him. Amram was too, but when he leaned over and kissed the top of my head, time returned to me. It was as if they'd never left. "Father is at home?" I asked them.

"Yes," Becher said. "We just left him. I'm sure he's wondering where you are. We're still wondering why you and your mother were hiding in the bushes."

Mother chewed on her lip. She wanted to tell Amram about the birth of Chaver and give him every glorious detail, be she couldn't while we were standing in the road. Instead, she embraced him, and I heard her whisper in his ear. "Go home. All is well. There you will find the Lord's promise to you."

To Becher she said, "Go with Amram. Atera is there as well."

Becher pulled Mother aside before we left. "Has there been any news of Eva?"

"Not yet," Mother replied softly. "Atera said she'll go to her tomorrow."

We walked home quickly, not mindful anymore about staying in the shadows. Av was waiting for us, and that was all we could think of. When we got to the door, it flung open, and he held out his arms. Em and I were lost in his embrace for a long time. None of us wanted to let go. His hair was grayer, and there were deep shadows beneath his eyes. I noticed that he winced when I hugged him. He recovered quickly, but it was too late. Mother and I had both seen the pain in his eyes.

Last night was the most wondrous of all nights. I was lulled to sleep by the soft whispers of my mother and father in the next room. It was like music to my ears. For several moons, I hadn't heard Father's voice. I hadn't felt his warm arms around me. I hadn't had the comfort of his love or his laughter. I didn't cry while he was away, but I've been crying with relief and joy since he returned. The page is damp with my tears, and I've rewritten many of my words because they were smudged.

Jochebed and Chaver consume my thoughts. Can this infant, with his tiny, red face and his toothless mouth, really deliver us from the bondage of the Egyptians? Em reminded me that all great leaders, even fierce ones like Pharaoh, were once small, helpless babies.

A Day Passes

My heart was filled with such gladness yesterday. Now it's weighted with sorrow. I was awakened in the night by voices, which drifted from the kitchen above my bedroom.

I climbed the stairs in the dark and peered around the corner. Av was sitting on a stool with his back hunched over and his head hung low. Mother dipped a rag into a basin of dark water. She wrung it out and tenderly patted his back with it.

Father held a clay lamp, and by its light I could

see the pain etched on his face. Each time Em touched the rag to his skin, the muscles in his cheek clenched "They are beasts that did this to you," she cried.

Father turned on his stool, and I saw the bloody wounds that striped his sunburned back. He put the lamp on the floor beside him and covered Mother's hands with his. "Please remember, Kezia, that we were the lucky ones, Becher, Amram, and I. There were many more who fell under the weight of the whip who didn't get up again."

Mother sobbed quietly. Her tears dripped into the basin of water that was stained with my father's blood. I'd heard it said that the store cities were built with the blood of our people. I didn't understand the meaning of those words until last night. I ran down the stairs. I don't think Mother and Father ever suspected I was there.

One Week Later

It's a comfort to hear Av and Becher in the workshop again. I hear their tools bump the wood of the table when they pick them up or put them down. I hear the clang of metal against stone when Father hammers the chisel. I hear the sigh of their stools when they move about. I'm even glad to hear their voices as they argue among themselves. These are all joyful sounds to my ears.

When Becher arrived this morning, he told us Atera had sent word to him. She was staying with Eva at a safe house because she had just delivered *two* babies! A boy and a girl! Becher is beside himself with joy and worry. Anyone with a baby boy in Goshen lives in continual fear.

Mother and I went to visit Chaver as we have done every day since his birth. As soon as we arrived, Miriam took my hand and led me into the storage room in the back. Chaver was content lying on his back.

"You can help me," she announced. "He has to be washed every day."

I loosened his cloths, and Miriam washed him with the water she'd warmed before I arrived. We rubbed him with olive oil and sprinkled dried myrtle leaves on his skin before we wrapped him up again. Then Miriam let me hold him.

In the span of only a week, I've become attached to Chaver. His head smells baby sweet, and his skin is warm and soft. I give him three kisses every time I leave him, one on each little cheek and one on his forehead.

Time to Plant!

Miriam and I walked to the river, something we haven't done in a quite a while. The planting season the Egyptians call Proyet has arrived. It's my favorite time of the year in Egypt. The dry, hot summer has been replaced by cool weather and gentle breezes. As predicted, the flood was excellent this year. The soil is ripe and fertile.

Farmers were tossing barley and wheat seeds into the ploughed earth today. Goats walked across the newly sewn fields and pressed the seeds farther into the soil, out of reach of watchful birds. The black kites, in particular, are the pirates of the sky. They swoop down and steal juicy treasures from the fields daily. Many times during harvest, children are sent out to jump up and down and wave long strips of cloth to chase the thieves away.

We stopped to watch a shepherd thread his flock through a shallow watercourse packed with water lettuce. Sheep and goats are fond of the water lettuce, and he allowed them to pause and feast on the lush leaves before he moved on to new pastureland farther east.

It was a good day, peaceful and serene, and I felt happy. Miriam didn't; she was quiet the whole afternoon. We sat on the grassy bank for a little while. Water lilies with spiked blue petals sunbathed on their green pads. They floated lazily past us on the river's slow current.

"What is it?" I pressed. "Are you worried about Chaver?"

"Not worried," she replied. "I know the Lord wouldn't call him if he didn't have a plan to care for him."

"Then what?"

Miriam sighed. "I'm not sure. I just feel uneasy. I can't explain it better than that."

We walked back in silence, holding hands. Father says he thinks the Lord has given Miriam a special gift, but she's still too young to understand what to do with it. I wish more than ever that life was fun and carefree the way it used to be. Miriam was right when she said a season of great change is upon us. There's too much sadness among our people in Goshen now.

I stopped to visit with Chaver before I returned home. I'm surprised at how much he's grown in one moon's time. His face is no longer red and wrinkled. Now it's the color of creamy buttermilk. Long, silky eyelashes frame his dark eyes, and he's quick to smile and laugh. I've seen many babies but never one as beautiful as Chaver.

Aaron is a good brother. He sits by Chaver for long stretches and makes silly faces. He even holds him gently on his lap and kisses his cheek in a noisy way, which makes his baby brother laugh.

My heart breaks for Chaver though, because he can't leave the house. Once in a while, Jochebed carries him into the tiny courtyard so he can feel the sun on his face and hear the whisper of the breeze. The Lord sends his songbirds to the fruit trees in the courtyard, and they tweet their sweetest lullabies.

Jochebed and Amram are aware that they can't hide him forever, but what can they do? They have no other choice but to live day to day, footstep by footstep. It's a lesson we're all learning.

A New Friend

Father was gone for several hours today, and Em was mysterious about his whereabouts. I asked where he went, and she smiled and said nothing. I asked when he would return, and she smiled and said nothing.

Three hours later another mystery was revealed. The door opened, and he walked in carrying a wooden cage covered in a scarlet cloth. Father laughed when he saw my face, and he pulled the cloth away to reveal a black kitten! It mewed pitifully, and its green eyes searched our faces. I ran to Av and took the cage from his hands.

"Why have you brought home a kitten?" I asked.

"We need a cat," he replied. "She'll keep away the rats and the snakes when she grows. I was lucky to find a litter at the market. The adults are mean, and I know you're afraid of them. Treat this one with tenderness, and she'll protect our house and be a loyal, gentle companion to you."

I took her out at once and held her close to my body. She was so tiny, I could fit her into the palm of one hand. Mother warmed a small bowl of goats' milk for her, and she drank with such eagerness, my heart was filled with pleasure. She said the poor thing was probably malnourished. I stroked her tiny head with my finger, and to my great surprise, she fell asleep within minutes. She'll need a proper name, but I must wait until I get to know her. A good name should fit its owner just right.

After Dinner

In a few hours' time, my kitten has revealed her name to me. She told me, by the way she frolics, that her name is Chanah, which means "grace-ful." Miriam came to call, and I hid Chanah in my pocket to surprise her. Horror spread across her face when she saw my tunic wiggle. I'm sure she thought a rat had slipped into my pocket in the night. Chanah peeked her head out and mewed in her characteristic way.

Miriam's eyes widened with delight. "When did you get a kitten?" she cried.

I pulled Chanah from my tunic and held her out for Miriam to hold. "Just today. Father brought her home. He said we need one to keep the vermin away." Chanah purred as Miriam ran her fingers along her soft back and beneath her chin.

"I want a kitten," Miriam murmured. "She's so sweet."

"You have a baby who is sweeter," I told her. "Your mother will never allow a cat in the house when the baby is so little. You can come over and play with Chanah anytime you want, just like I go to your house and play with Chaver."

Several Weeks Later

Trouble is brewing again. For many weeks, we didn't see any Egyptians among us, and there were no more tales of babies drowning in the river. We thought the danger was over, that perhaps the pharaoh had decided to leave us alone. We were wrong.

Last night one of our safe houses was raided. Luckily, there were no babies there at the time. Just that morning, the mothers had felt safe enough to return to their homes. Em said it was an act of the Lord that saved them. Why else would the mothers decide to take their babies home on the very day the Egyptians raided the safe house?

As Chaver grows, he's learning to exercise his vocal cords. He likes to talk and laugh, and when Miriam sings, as she always does, he opens his mouth and gurgles with might. Jochebed is more worried than ever. We all are.

An Adventure!

A river hunt was organized among the men yesterday, and Miriam and I were allowed to join the fun. Of course, we didn't hunt, but we walked along and took great pleasure in watching the folly.

Chanah has grown. Although she's a tiny cat by nature, she's already proved herself to be a capable hunter! Several rats have turned up dead at the foot of my bed mat. Em said she killed them to please me and then offered them as a gift. The first time I awoke with a rat by my bed, I stepped on it. Mother said she'd never heard such a scream in her life. She and Father ran into my room, and Chanah flew out the window.

Now I open one eye and look all around my bed before I get up. If there's a rat, I holler to Father and won't move until he takes it away. Then I scratch Chanah's head and say, "Good little hunter!"

Father and twenty other men gathered near the river marshes. Several cats, including my Chanah, were held until the men were ready. When the signal was given, the cats were let go. They scampered through tall reeds and grasses. When the birds flew from the brush in a wild flurry of feathers, the men flung lassos, throwsticks, and weighed ropes into the air. Arrows flew from taut bows.

All in all, I counted two geese, seven ducks, three herons, a pelican, and a crane. Miriam and I left after the first round, but the men continued their hunt for several more hours, moving steadily down the river.

When Father returned later, Chanah wasn't with him. She didn't come home until the dead of the night. I know because she jumped to the window ledge and yowled in the moonlight. Her eyes glowed green. I think she was proud of herself and wanted everyone to know.

Another Delivery

This afternoon there was a peculiar knock at the door. It was delivered in a musical pattern like the one several months ago, so I wasn't surprised to see the man called Pelet at the door. He shifted from one foot to the other and glanced over his shoulder several times. "I've come to inquire about a seal. Is your father at home?"

"Yes, of course." I beckoned him to come in and led him into Av's workshop. He and Father whispered for several minutes before Pelet saw himself to the door. Father talked with Em, and this time they didn't hide the conversation from me. Pelet had gotten word that there would be another Egyptian raid in about seven days. This time our houses would be targeted.

Father wanted to alert Amram and Jochebed, but Em put her hand on his arm. She warned him to wait a discreet amount of time in case Pelet was followed. Av paced back and forth, then walked back into his workshop to tinker with his tools. I heard him praying, and after a short while he left.

A Secret Meeting ~ Nightfall

I have solemn news to share. Earlier in the evening, we were summoned to Amram and Jochebed's house and ushered into the storage room in the back. Becher and Atera had been invited and had already arrived. Hoshaiah, I noticed on my way in, was in the courtyard. Amram apologized but reminded us that the windowless storage room was the safest room in the house.

I squeezed between Miriam and Aaron. Chanah is too big now to fit into my pocket, but I carried her with me. She was gracious enough to allow Aaron to pet her before she took off in pursuit of interesting prey. Chaver was asleep on Jochebed's lap.

"Do you know what your father is going to tell us?" I asked Miriam.

She nodded. "He told Mother and me before you arrived." Her eyes were downcast, and I was about to ask her what was wrong, but we were interrupted.

Amram lifted Chaver from Jochebed's arms. The baby's long eyelashes fluttered, but his eyes didn't open. "I've spent restless nights deep in prayer," he murmured. "I know beyond all doubt that our God, for reasons beyond our understanding, has chosen this innocent to deliver our people." He stroked Chaver's cheek.

"However, events of recent days make me tremble for his safety. If our deception is discovered now, the king's wrath will be so great, I will be slaughtered at once and Chaver will be drowned. He will carry to his grave God's promise of deliverance.

"After much prayer and petition," Amram continued, "I have determined that I can no longer take matters into my own hands and hide my son. I must surrender my fear and commit Chaver to God's care."

Father's breath whistled through his parted lips. Becher cleared his throat. Em and Atera stared at one another.

"Tomorrow," Amram said solemnly, "we will make a sturdy cradle of bulrushes pulled from the river's edge. Chaver will be placed inside and sent adrift in Iteru."

Mother gasped and put her hands to her chest. The color drained from her face like milk emptied from a jug.

"It would appear that I am offering my son to the river as the king desires, but I am not. I am surrendering my son to God." Amram placed the sleepy Chaver back in his mother's arms. "Our father Abraham trusted the Lord so much, he was willing to give his son as an offering. I trust that the same God who did not allow harm to befall Isaac will protect my son better than I can. He has the means to keep him safe so that he might serve him and fulfill a greater good."

I hope I've chronicled the meeting well. Amram's words are burned into my memory and aren't easy to forget. Chills run through me as I recall them. I've never heard such words of faith in my life. Mother and Father have told me the stories of our forefathers, Abraham and Isaac, but I've never seen an example of such faith in my lifetime until now. Father said Amram's courage is extraordinary.

Everyone was silent afterwards. What was there to say? I saw peace in Jochebed's eyes and in Miriam's. Miriam asked me to help her gather the bulrushes from the river in the morning, and I agreed.

The Next Day

The pyramids were silhouetted beneath a pink sky when Miriam, Chanah, and I walked to the river. Egyptian children were already playing naked at the water's edge, some standing ankle deep, washing themselves. A grove of papyrus plants, at least six cubits high, grew close to the shore here, so Miriam and I kicked off our sandals. We tucked the hems of our long tunics into our belts to make short skirts, and then we waded into the warm river. Startled frogs hopped from their hiding spot among the reeds.

We reached into the water among small, darting fish and grasped the bottom of a stem near the muddy bottom. We jiggled it back and forth to loosen it from its roots. This proved to be more temptation than Chanah could resist. Crouching low, she moved her head from left to right, her eyes on the swaying stalk. She crept closer on her belly until her instincts screamed, and she jumped from the shore to the tall reed. Her claws dug into the tough stalk, and she swung wildly in the air until we pulled the reed loose and she plopped into the water.

Chanah swam to shore, shook herself off, and gave me a look that spelled both disappointment and disgust. She ran off, soggy and depressed. Despite the sad task we were undertaking, Miriam and I laughed. Chanah has brought me joy since Father brought her home.

When we'd gathered enough papyrus to make a thick bundle, we hoisted the tall plants over each of our shoulders and carried them back to Miriam's house.

It's easy to gaze at the lazy river and think it serene or gentle, but it's not. I tossed and turned in my bed last night thinking about Chaver. When I awoke, my thoughts dwelled on the crocodiles and hippos that lie in wait beneath the surface of the water. The river I love so much now represents danger and evil to me.

Miriam and I sat in the courtyard for hours as we watched Jochebed prepare the papyrus. She fashioned it into a small, compact boat just large enough to hold a baby. I wondered what she was thinking, knowing that her hands were making the boat that would carry her infant son downriver.

Chaver rested in Miriam's arms, his eyes following the songbirds that fluttered between the trees. Chanah stretched beside me in the warmth of the sun. Her eyes followed the songbirds too, but I don't think her thoughts were so pure.

I picked up the top of a papyrus plant, which resembles a crown of hair. Jochebed had discarded the tops in a pile. I lightly brushed Chaver's face and neck with it, and he giggled when it tickled his skin.

We stayed while Jochebed carried a clay bowl to the river to scoop fresh mud from the bottom. When she returned, she dipped her hands into it and smeared it over the small boat. The minerals in the mud created a seal that would keep the river water from seeping into the boat.

"When is the time?" I asked Miriam softly. I couldn't bring myself to say, "At what time will Chaver sail down Iteru?"

"I don't know," she murmured. "As soon as

Father says it's time, I suppose. The mud has to dry for several hours, so I think they may want to wait until tomorrow or the next day. It's best for Chaver to float in the daylight anyway."

"But where will Chaver float to?" As soon as the words left my mouth, I regretted them. It was a stupid, careless thing to ask her. "I'm sorry, Miriam, I—"

"Laila, it's all right," she interrupted. There was kindness in her eyes when she looked at me. "I have the same thoughts. I know you love Chaver. We're more like family than friends. I suppose we must trust that he'll float into God's care. That's what Mother told me last night. She said angels from heaven will close the jaws of the hippopotamuses and the crocodiles so they can't hurt him. She said they'll tuck Chaver beneath their wide wings so no danger can befall him."

I'm comforted by Miriam's words. Like Amram said, we must surrender our fear and commit Chaver to God's care. I wish it were easier to do.

Two Days Pass ~ Chaver and the Princess

I'm filled with emotion. Every time I begin to write, my eyes cloud with tears and I must wipe them away and begin again. Last night Miriam came to the house, and we went into the courtyard to talk.

"Come to the river before sunup," she told me. "Mother and I will wait at the place where we gathered the bulrushes." She turned to leave, but I grabbed her arm.

"Is it time?" I asked. She nodded, and I felt fear rise up in my throat. It tasted bitter and vile. I believe Amram is a godly man, but I couldn't help wondering if he had made a terrible mistake. What if it wasn't God's will for him to send Chaver to the river? All I could think of was *what if* . . .

Miriam saw the fear in me, and she pulled me to the bench by the willow tree. I watched as she pulled her necklace from her neck. I'd made the necklace for her several years ago from a piece of chipped lapis lazuli. I wasn't supposed to have polished it without Father's help, and when I did, it broke in two.

Father hadn't reprimanded me. He knew my tears reflected my shame. He took the two pieces and made two necklaces for me instead. I gave one to Miriam, and I kept the other. They became our friendship necklaces, and until today, neither of us had ever taken them off.

"This necklace is my most prized possession," she told me. "Will you do something for me without asking any questions?"

"Yes, yes," I told her. "You know I'd do anything."

"All right, then," she replied. "I want you to take care of it for me. It's important that you keep it safe."

I didn't understand why Miriam would ask me to care for the necklace, but I'd agreed not to ask any questions, so I didn't. I waited for her to give it to me, but she didn't move. The breeze stirred the willow, and the leaves rustled against one another. She looked away.

I held out my hand to her, but I saw Miriam's fingers grip the necklace even tighter. "I'll take care of it for you," I reassured her. "Don't worry. I won't let anything happen to it."

She bound the cord together and tucked it beside the lapis lazuli in a tight bundle in the palm of her hand. "Laila, are you sure you're willing to keep it safe? Are you sure you *can*?" Her eyes were desperate now, and I was confused and frustrated. Didn't she trust me?

"I'll take good care of it, Miriam," I repeated, "but I can't do anything until you give it to me."

She lifted two fingers so that I could see the brilliant blue of the stone, and she moved her hand toward me. "Yes, you're right. I'm sorry. Here," she offered.

I reached out to take it from her hand, and when I did she snatched it back.

"Miriam!" I was shocked at her odd behavior. "If you don't trust me, why did you ask me to care for it in the first place?"

"I want you to take care of it, Laila," she admitted. "But I don't think I can give it to you." Her dark eyes bore into mine, waiting for me to respond.

"Then I can't take care of it," I told her. "If you keep it, you must assume responsibility for it."

Miriam smiled at me. Her face was luminescent in the moonlight. She reached over and opened up my palm and placed the necklace inside of it. "Laila, forgive me, but this was a lesson Father taught me last night. Fear gripped me just like it gripped you. I saw it in your eyes, and Father saw it in mine. He showed me that if we don't commit our treasures to God's care, how can he care for them for us? Do we trust him or not? You couldn't take care of my necklace until I released it and gave it to you. As long as I held on to it, there was nothing you could do for me."

I felt peace wash over me. I understood. "Chaver is our treasure," I said. "If we don't release him into God's care, then God can't take care of him. If we continue to hold on to him, than we must assume responsibility for him."

"Yes!" Miriam exclaimed. "Now I must go. I've been here too long already. It's not safe. I want you to keep my necklace as a reminder of the lesson both of us have learned. Give it back to me when you know the time is right."

I'm not sure what time Miriam was referring to, but I suppose I'll know soon enough.

Many Things Have Happened

I awoke well before dawn and was surprised to learn that Av and Em had been awake for several hours. All night, they said, they heard footsteps outside our door. Father went outside to check several times, but there was no one there. This morning he found footprints in the moist soil beneath our windows. "Danger lurks," he said. "It's good that Chaver will be committed to God's care soon. They're searching for him."

The full moon lit my path to the river. I thought as I walked. I saw Miriam and Jochebed waiting. The papyrus basket was already closed and hidden in the tall reeds. "He's sleeping," Miriam whispered. The water lapped against the tiny boat and rocked it gently.

Jochebed bent down and put her hand on the

basket. "I commit you, Chaver, son of Amram, to the Lord's care." She nudged the boat until it was within the current's grasp.

"Go," she told Miriam. "Stay close to the reeds and don't let Chaver out of your sight. Come back and tell me where the Lord has delivered him."

Miriam and I took off our sandals and lifted our hems as we'd done two days before. We waded among the thick, tall reeds, which hid us when the sun rose and the sky was lit again. Every time I lifted my foot, I wondered if I would lose it in the jaws of a crocodile, but I saw none on this day. The river cradled the basket close to its shallow edge, never pushing it into deeper water.

We waded like this for several hours, resting when Chaver's boat snagged on a reed, moving when the current pulled it free. I had no idea where we were until Miriam held out her arm and pointed. "Stop, Laila. We have to stop here," she said.

I scanned the riverbank and saw the golden columns of the palace. Once again I tasted fear in my throat. I'd been so busy watching the river and the basket, I hadn't realized we were this close.

"Miriam! We have to get Chaver. He's floating too close to the palace." I waded farther into the water and tried to reach the basket, but the water was pushing against my legs, slowing me down. Miriam was gripping my shoulder and trying to pull me back when we heard voices. We ducked and tried to hide among the grasses.

The voices of girls playing and laughing were getting closer. "Come on," Miriam urged. "We must leave Chaver."

I was wearing Miriam's pendant as well my own, and I felt the two stones bounce against the hollow of my neck. I reached up and stroked them with my thumb and was reminded of her words—*"Chaver is our treasure. If we don't release him into God's care, then God can't take care of him."*

I followed her out of the river, and we crept to the same grove of eucalyptus and tamarisk trees we'd hidden in before. Several slave girls wearing simple white tunics were walking along the river's edge. They tossed a ball back and forth. My heart trembled when I saw Chaver's basket drift nearer to them.

The princess sat on the low wall that separated the shallow pool from the river. She was dressed in a white, pleated sheath similar to the one she'd worn before, but this time it was pulled up to her knees, and her feet dangled in the water. Her hair was glossy black, and her eyes were rimmed with black kohl. Her lips and her cheeks were stained red. She was laughing as she watched her slave girls play.

Miriam and I watched the basket as it bobbed among the reeds. Suddenly the ball flew into the river and landed in front of the basket. Miriam inhaled sharply, and I bit my lip. I didn't feel the pain, but I tasted the blood as it trickled into my mouth.

The girls stopped playing, and they stared at the basket. The princess leaned forward and moved her head to one side. Then Chaver began to whimper. Miriam turned toward me with wet eyes and motioned with her hand toward the river's edge. We crawled into the reeds again and hid. We watched, and we waited.

"There! There's something there beside the

ball!" The princess pointed to the basket. "One of you girls, bring it to me." A tall, dark girl waded into the water and lifted the basket into her arms. She climbed onto the bank and set the basket on the low wall beside the princess.

I watched the king's daughter look inside, and I saw her eyebrows lift in surprise. "This is one of the Hebrew babies," she said.

My chest felt tight as she lifted Chaver out. I wanted to run and snatch him from her hands. She stroked his cheek and studied him. "He's like a son of the gods," she murmured. "I've never seen a baby so beautiful." Chaver was crying, and when she held him close to her bosom, he cried louder. His body was trembling now, and his face was red.

"This child is hungry," she called to the slave girls. "Bring me a wet nurse to feed him at once."

Miriam stood up. We were only a stone's throw away from the princess, and I tried to pull her back down. "It will be in vain, Princess, for an Egyptian woman to try to feed a Hebrew child!" she called out.

The princess looked up. She gazed at Miriam with wide, startled eyes.

"If you so desire," Miriam continued boldly. "I would be obliged to find a Hebrew wet nurse whom the baby will surely feed from."

I thought at first that the princess hadn't heard or hadn't understood. She said nothing for a long moment but continued to stare at Miriam.

Then she smiled. "Yes, go. Go and find a Hebrew woman for me."

The Truth

Would this story seem untrue if I were to write that Chaver is back in Jochebed's arms? I swear it to be the truth. Miriam and I ran the entire way home and found Jochebed and Amram sitting with Mother, Father, Atera, and Becher.

"Mother! Come at once. The princess has saved Chaver, and she wants a Hebrew woman to nurse him!"

Jochebed came with us. The princess was walking along the shore, looking in the direction we'd left. I'm sure she was waiting for us. She was rocking Chaver in her arms, but I heard his cries from a long way off. Jochebed reached out for him, and the king's daughter placed him in her arms.

She watched Jochebed nurse him, and she observed the familiar way she held him, but she said nothing of it. The princess nodded, satisfied. "I drew this child out of the water, and I will call him Moses. Take this baby for a time and nurse him for me, and I will pay you."

The palace shone behind us as we walked slowly back home.

In less than one day, Chaver was set afloat in the wilds of the river Iteru, he drifted into the arms of a beautiful Egyptian princess who saved his life, and he was returned to his mother. One day, Jochebed said, she'll have to surrender him to the palace. When that day comes, he won't be far away from us, and he'll always be safe.

I took off Miriam's necklace and hung it around her neck where it belonged. "It's the right time," I told her. "I've learned an important lesson, one I'll never forget."

I've learned to give my treasures to God, and I know that he is faithful to care for them. Amram surrendered his son to God's care, and then God directed his footsteps one step at a time. The Lord not only protected his treasure but blessed him and his family for their faith and their obedience.

So many thoughts come to me now as I write. I remember the first time Miriam and I went to the palace. She told me she felt peaceful because it appeared that the princess was a kind woman. I wondered then what she meant by that and why she even cared.

Mother told me once that Miriam possessed a gift that would mature in her as she grew. Tonight when I told her what happened at the river, she said she was convinced that Miriam was a spokeswoman for God. He had used her to speak to the princess! She said it's a rare and special gift.

Miriam has another gift. It's the gift of song. How her voice has warmed my heart and filled me with joy. I may not have the voice of an angel, and I may not be blessed with a bold spirit, but my best friend has taught me that my quiet, practical ways are unique and special to me.

I've been able to record this amazing story of faith and love and courage. Miriam said to me, "What would this story be if no one knew about it? If there was no one who could write it down so future generations could be inspired by it?"

I had a sudden thought and decided to ask her. "Do you think we'll be alive when God uses Chaver to deliver our people from Egypt?"

She smiled. "If we are, I know you'll be carrying your pen and paper, recording every detail of it!"

I hope she's right.

Epilogue

Jochebed nursed Chaver until he was old enough to be taken to the royal court of Pharaoh. There he was called Moses and would be called this name for the rest of his life. He was educated beside royal heirs of princes who came to Egypt to be trained in the sciences, literature, writing, and all manner of higher learning.

During these early years, Miriam and Laila often followed the river to the palace, where they hid in a grove of trees. They waited to catch a glimpse of the royal heir they had once bathed and held in their arms.

Moses the prince lived at the palace for forty years. It is unknown whether he visited his birth family during this time. The plight of his people stirred his heart when he watched two Hebrews slaves beaten by a fellow Egyptian. He killed the Egyptian taskmaster and fled Egypt. Moses the shepherd spent the next forty years in solitude in the wilderness of Midian.

Eighty years after Moses's birth, God sent Aaron, now an anointed prophet, into the desert to be reunited with his brother. They returned to Egypt, and together they implored Pharaoh to free the Hebrews.

The word that the Lord had spoken to Amram came to pass. Moses the deliverer led his people out of bondage in Egypt, where they had dwelled for more than four hundred years. Aaron, as well as his sister Miriam, who was ninety-two years old, accompanied him.

Following the miraculous parting of the Red Sea, Moses composed a song, which some say is the oldest recorded song in the world. Miriam used her gift as a songstress, and she and Moses led the Israelites in a joyous song of victory. Under her leadership, the women accompanied the music with timbrels and dancing.

More than a year after the Israelites left Egypt, Aaron and Miriam began to murmur against their brother Moses. The Bible says the anger of the Lord burned against them, and Miriam was struck with leprosy. Aaron pleaded with Moses on her behalf, and Moses pleaded to the Lord, "O God, please heal her!" Miriam was healed, but she was forced to leave the camp for seven days.

As a consequence of their disobedience, the Israelites wandered in the wilderness an additional forty years. No member of the original generation that left Egypt was allowed to enter the Promised Land.

Miriam lived to be 132 years old. She died in the wilderness and was buried at Kadesh. Aaron died at the age of 123 atop Mount Hor in the presence of Moses and his son Eleazar. When the Israelites learned of his death, they mourned for thirty days. He was known thereafter as "the saint of the Lord."

Not long after the death of his sister and brother, Moses climbed Mount Nebo, where God told him, "This is the land I promised on oath to Abraham, Isaac and Jacob when I said, 'I will give it to your descendants.' I have let you see it with your eyes, but you will not cross over into it."

Moses was 120 when he died in Moab. It has been said that God, with the help of heavenly angels, buried his body and hid his grave. To this day, no one knows the location of his burial site. The Israelites wept and mourned for thirty days.

Amram lived to be 137 years old, but little else is known of his life or that of his wife, Jochebed. Laila was ninety-two when she left Egypt. She was married, with three grown children. Her mother and father and Atera and Becher did not live to see Moses deliver them from their oppressors, though they always believed he would.

When Laila was camped with the Israelites beneath the mountain of God, she was reminded of how her father had described it to her as a young girl. Several times she watched God descend upon the peak in a fury of clouds, fire, and thunder. She was never happier, and she recorded every detail just like Miriam had said she would.

Laila died in the wilderness not long after her husband but a year before Miriam. They had remained best friends their whole lives. Miriam wrapped up her friend's scrolls and stored them in clay vessels. She gave them to Laila's children and instructed them not to open the jars until after she died.

One year later Joshua led the new generation of Israelites into the Promised Land. Laila's children remembered their mother's diaries. They pried off the lid and carefully pulled them out. The scrolls were tied with leather cords from which hung two jagged pendants of lapis lazuli.

The Song of Moses and Miriam

I will sing to the LORD,
    for he is highly exalted.
The horse and its rider
    he has hurled into the sea.
The LORD is my strength and my song;
    he has become my salvation.
He is my God, and I will praise him,
    my father's God, and I will exalt him.
The LORD is a warrior;
    the LORD is his name.
Pharaoh's chariots and his army
    he has hurled into the sea.
The best of Pharaoh's officers
    are drowned in the Red Sea.
The deep waters have covered them;
    they sank to the depths like a stone.

Your right hand, O LORD,
    was majestic in power.
Your right hand, O LORD,
    shattered the enemy,
In the greatness of your majesty
    you threw down those who opposed you.

You unleashed your burning anger;
  it consumed them like stubble.
By the blast of your nostrils
  the waters piled up.
The surging waters stood firm like a wall;
  the deep waters congealed in the heart of
    the sea.

The enemy boasted,
  "I will pursue, I will overtake them.
I will divide the spoils;
  I will gorge myself on them.
I will draw my sword
  and my hand will destroy them."
But you blew with your breath,
  and the sea covered them.
They sank like lead
  in the mighty waters.

Who among the gods is like you, O LORD?
  Who is like you—
  majestic in holiness,
  awesome in glory,
  working wonders?
You stretched out your right hand
  and the earth swallowed them.

In your unfailing love you will lead
    the people you have redeemed.
In your strength you will guide them
    to your holy dwelling.
The nations will hear and tremble;
    anguish will grip the people of Philistia.
The chiefs of Edom will be terrified,
    the leaders of Moab will be seized with
      trembling,
the people of Canaan will melt away;
    terror and dread will fall upon them.
By the power of your arm
    they will be as still as a stone—
until your people pass by, O LORD,
    until the people you bought pass by.
You will bring them in and plant them
    on the mountain of your inheritance—
the place, O LORD, you made for your
    dwelling,
    the sanctuary, O LORD, your
      hands established.
The LORD will reign
    for ever and ever.

                    Exodus 15:1–18

This oil painting, by Simeon Solomon, shows Jochebed as she cuddles Moses. Young Miriam, looking on, holds the basket that will carry her infant brother down the Nile.

The island of Philae, pictured here, was located at the beginning of the Nile's first cataract. It was covered with monu-
ments dedicated to various gods and goddesses. The most
important one was the great temple built for the winged goddess Isis.

Merchant ships from surrounding countries, like Phoenicia and Nubia, frequently made stops along the Nile. They traded their goods for Egyptian papyrus, linen, and even gold. In return, Egypt received exotic merchandise like monkeys, horses, and leopard skins.

With the help of a "shadoof," Egyptians used river water to irrigate their crops. In its earliest form, a pole was weighted on one end with a stone. A pot, attached to the other end, was lowered into the water and easily pulled up. In this photograph, taken in more modern times, a more sophisticated shadoof can be seen.

Throughout the centuries, Bible characters have inspired
and captured the imagination of great artists. Gothic sculptor
Giovanni Pisano was one of those. It is believed he created
this statue of Miriam in northern Italy, where he worked.

This lithograph, by Charles Edmund Brock, depicts Moses pulled from the Nile by one of the royal handmaidens. Miriam is shown boldly standing at the river's edge, gazing into the eyes of the Egyptian princess.

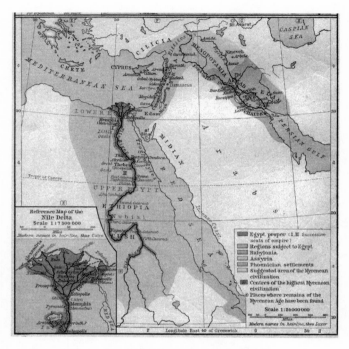

A map of the ancient Orient, including Egypt and the
Nile Delta

Laila's Home

The story takes place in the land of Goshen in Egypt's northeastern Nile Delta region. It is set in the years 1527 to 1526 BC.

The People Laila Wrote of Most

Miriam:	Older sister of Moses and Aaron
Herself:	Miriam's best friend *
Chaver/Moses:	Miriam's youngest brother, the deliverer of the Israelites
Father/Izri/Av:	Laila's father *
Mother/Kezia/Em:	Laila's mother *
Jochebed:	Miriam's mother
Amram:	Miriam's father
Becher:	Close friend of Laila's family, Atera's huband *

Atera:	Close friend of Laila's family, Becher's wife *
Shiphrah:	Egyptian midwife
Puah:	Egyptian midwife

Note: Most Bible scholars believe the two midwives who tended to Moses were of Egyptian descent but are called "Hebrew midwives" in the Bible because they tended to the Hebrews.

The People Laila Encountered
(in order of appearance)

Pharaoh:	King of Egypt
Aaron:	Miriam's younger brother
Bernice:	Pregnant woman *
Elias:	Bernice's husband *
Pharaoh's daughter:	The princess who pulled Moses from the water and adopted him

Eva: Atera and Becher's daughter *

Pelet: Messenger *

Helsa: Pregnant women who gives birth
in a safe house *

* denotes fictional characters

Tracing History: A Timeline

1898 BC
Joseph is taken to Egypt on a slave caravan. He is sold to Potiphar, an officer of Pharaoh.

1885 BC
Joseph proves himself so intelligent and trustworthy, he is made chief ruler of Egypt—second only to Pharaoh.

1876 BC
Jacob and his sons reunite with Joseph, and Pharaoh welcomes them into Egypt.

1859 BC
Jacob dies. He is embalmed in Egyptian fashion and taken by Joseph and a small convoy of Egyptian soldiers to Canaan. He is buried in the

cave of Machpelah with Sarah, Abraham, Isaac, Rebekah, and Leah.

1805 BC
Joseph dies. His bones are carried back to Canaan and buried in a plot of land owned by his father, Jacob.

1526 BC
Moses is born to Amram and Jochebed. Aaron is three years old at the time. Miriam is twelve.

1446 BC
Moses leads the Israelites out of Egypt.

1406 BC
Miriam, Aaron, and Moses all die in the wilderness. Not long after, Joshua leads the Israelites into Canaan, the Promised Land.

Goshen's Place in History

The land of Goshen was sometimes referred to as the "field of Zoan" or the "land of Rameses." It was a relatively small area of about nine hundred square miles, located in Egypt's northeastern delta along the ancient Nile River. Due to the annual flooding of the Nile, the delta, a triangle-shaped piece of land located at the mouth of the river, was the most fertile area in all of ancient Africa.

Vineyards, balsam plantations, gardens, orchards, and fields were spread from end to end. Its rich topsoil was between fifty and seventy-five feet deep. Canals were built to harness the river water and irrigate the crops planted farther inland.

Nine years after Joseph was appointed prime minister of Egypt, he was reunited with his father, Jacob, and his brothers. He invited them to join him in his new country:

Then Joseph said to his brothers and to his father's household, "I will go up and speak to Pharaoh and will say to him, 'My brothers and my father's household, who were living in the land of Canaan, have come to me. The men are shepherds; they tend livestock, and they have brought along their flocks and herds and everything they own.' When Pharaoh calls you in and asks, 'What is your occupation?' you should answer, 'Your servants have tended livestock from our boyhood on, just as our fathers did.' Then you will be allowed to settle in the region of Goshen, for all shepherds are detestable to the Egyptians.

Genesis 46:31–34

Jacob agreed to move his family to Egypt if they were allowed to live apart from the Egyptians. They were, and they settled in the area known to them as Goshen. The delta was so productive that when Egypt endured a seven-year famine following Jacob's entry into Egypt, there was enough food and water stored in reserve to last the duration. The Israelites lived in Goshen for 430 years, part of that time in peace and part of it in subservience to the Egyptians:

> Then a new king, who did not know about Joseph, came to power in Egypt. "Look," he said to his people, "the Israelites have become much too numerous for us. Come, we must deal shrewdly with them or they will become even more numerous and, if war breaks out, will join our enemies, fight against us and leave the country."
>
> So they put slave masters over them to oppress them with forced labor, and they built Pithom and Rameses as store cities for Pharaoh.
>
> Exodus 1:8–11

The fortress cities of Pithom and Rameses, which the Israelites were forced to build, served as garrisons, which helped defend Egypt's borders from Asian attacks. They also served as bases from which the Egyptians could launch attacks against Syria and Palestine.

The land of Goshen was said to be so beautiful and the food so plentiful that the Israelites were to quick to forget the bondage they had endured there. After Moses led them out of Egypt in search of the Promised Land, they complained continually of the land they had left behind:

> The whole Israelite community set out from Elim and came to the Desert of Sin, which is between Elim and Sinai, on the fifteenth day of the second month after they had come out of Egypt. In the desert the whole community grumbled against Moses and Aaron. The Israelites said to them, "If only we had died by the LORD's hand in Egypt! There we sat around pots of meat and ate all the food we wanted, but you have brought us out into this desert to starve this entire assembly to death."
>
> Exodus 16:1–3

Then and Now

The Nile River, also called Iteru in ancient times, was the longest river in the world. It flowed northward for about 4,300 miles from east central Africa through Uganda, Sudan, and Egypt to the Great Sea. It was the principal river of Africa and Egypt and was so essential to the people's existence that Egypt was even called the "gift of the Nile."

It was along the banks of the ancient Nile that some of the earliest forms of civilization emerged. Its waters gave life to the great Sahara Desert in northern Africa and the red land, or desert, of Egypt, which covered more than 90 percent of the country. Most Egyptians lived on the riverbanks, called the black land, beside the canals.

Each year Egyptians anxiously awaited the flooding of the Nile. To measure the river's rise and fall, they invented a unit of measurement called a nilometer. This instrument, usually a stone with horizontal lines, helped them predict whether to expect a high Nile year and flooding or a low Nile year and drought. Flooding in the Nile Delta in lower Egypt brought rich sediment over the banks, which created a top soil ideal for crops. The delta region has long been regarded as one of the most fertile areas in the world.

Along the banks and in the irrigated valleys, Egyptians planted wheat and barley and grew vegetables, fruit, and flax, which was used to make linen. They grazed sheep, goats, and cattle, particularly in the eastern delta. Papyrus plants from the river were used to make paper. Prior to the invention of papyrus paper, pottery shards were often used to write on. Since the Nile flowed north but the winds blew south, sailors could travel in either direction fairly easily between rapids.

In ancient times the Nile Delta had as many as seven tributaries. Today there are only two main branches, the Damietta and Rosetta. About 105 million people currently live along the Nile, most of them in Egypt. It is still regarded as the source of life for Africa. It can be breathtakingly beautiful, and many visitors cruise the river in feluccas or Nile river boats. In many places the Nile appears tame and friendly. Other parts remain mostly unnavigable and are wild, swarming with crocodiles and snakes.

Bibliography

Many sources were consulted and used in research for writing Laila and Miriam's story in the Promised Land Diaries series, including:

Adam Clarke's Commentary on the Bible, Adam Clarke, abridged by Ralph H. Earle (World Bible Publishing Co., 1996).

Atlas of the Bible: An Illustrated Guide to the Holy Land, edited by Joseph L. Gardner (Readers Digest Association, 1981).

The Bible as History, 2nd revised edition, Werner Keller, translated by William Neil; Joachim Rehork, translated by B. H Rasmussen (Bantam Books, 1982).

The Biblical Times, edited by Derek Williams (Baker Publishing Group, 1997).

Holman Bible Atlas, Thomas V. Brisco (Broadman & Holman Publishers, 1998).

Holman Book of Biblical Charts, Maps, and Reconstructions, edited by Marsha A. Ellis Smith (Broadman & Holman Publishers, 1993).

Jamieson, Fausset, and Brown's Commentary on the Whole Bible, Fausset, Brown, and Robert Jamieson (Zondervan Publishing House, 1999).

Matthew Henry's Commentary on the Whole Bible: Complete and Unabridged in One Volume, Matthew Henry (Hendrickson Publishers, 1991).

Meredith's Book of Bible Lists, J. L. Meredith (Bethany House Publishers, 1980).

Nelson's Illustrated Encyclopedia of the Bible, edited by John Drane (Thomas Nelson, Inc., 2001).

Nelson's New Illustrated Bible Manners & Customs, Howard F. Vos (Thomas Nelson Publishers, 1999).

The New International Dictionary of the Bible, edited by J. D. Douglas and Merrill C. Tenney (Zondervan Publishing House, 1987).

The Picture Bible Dictionary, Berkeley and Alvera Mickelsen (Chariot Books, an imprint of David C. Cook Publishing Co., 1993).

Women of the Bible: A One-Year Devotional Study of Women in Scripture, Ann Spangler and Jean Syswerda (Zondervan Publishing House, 1999).

The Works of Josephus, Complete and Unabridged, new updated edition, Flavius Josephus, translated by William Whiston (Hendrickson Publishers, Inc., 1980).

About the Author

Anne Tyra Adams is the author of more than a dozen children's books, several of which have been translated into three foreign languages: Indonesian, Korean, and Afrikaans. Two of her books, *The New Kids Book of Bible Facts* and *The Baker Book of Bible Travels for Kids*, provided the foundation for writing this series, the Promised Land Diaries.

A journalist and detailed researcher, Adams is also a "student of ancient history," with a deep fascination for the Jewish culture. She used all this experience, love of history, and curiosity to write this book.

When not working on more Promised Land Diaries, Adams loves to read the classics and ancient history, taking many armchair travels in time to foreign lands. She especially loves reading biographies of famous authors.

She and her husband and their two children live in Phoenix, Arizona. They often hike in the mountainous desert surrounding their home and have been known to spot quail, coyote, an occasional fox, and many lizards. Not to be outdone by the great outdoors, they share their home with three dogs, a cat, and an assortment of little fish.

The author would like to express
her deepest appreciation to Michael J. Ward,
director of TravelHistory.org,
Robin Stolfi and Jennifer Belt
of Art Resource, and Caroline Jennings
of the Bridgeman Art Library.

Permissions

Page 150: The Mother of Moses
c. 1860 (oil on canvas) by Simeon Solomon (1840–1905)
Delaware Art Museum, Wilmington, USA/Bequest of Robert Louis
Isaacson/Bridgeman Art Library

Page 151: The Islands of Philae on the Nile
Courtesy TravelHistory.org and the University of California
Libraries

Page 152: On the Blue Nile
Courtesy TravelHistory.org and the University of California
Libraries

Page153: Egyptians Drawing Nile Water for Irrigation
Courtesy TravelHistory.org and the University of California
Libraries

Page 154: Miriam, sister of Moses. Close-up of head.
Giovanni Pisano (1248–c.1314)
Location: Museo dell'Opera Metropolitana, Siena, Italy
Photo Credit: Alinari/Art Resource, NY

Page 155: Miriam Ventured to Come Closer
Illustration from *Through the Bible*, Venture Publishing
1928 (color litho) by Charles Edmund Brock (1870–1938)
Private Collection, Bridgeman Art Library

Page 156: Map of ancient Africa and the Nile Delta
Perry-Castaneda Library Map Collection
The University of Texas at Austin

Books in

THE PROMISED LAND DIARIES

Series

1

Persia's Brightest Star
The Diary of Queen Esther's Attendant

2

The Laughing Princess of the Desert
The Diary of Sarah's Traveling Companion

3

Priceless Jewel at the Well
The Diary of Rebekah's Nursemaid

4

The Peaceful Warrior
The Diary of Deborah's Armor Bearer

5

Songbird of the Nile
The Diary of Miriam's Friend

6

Beauty in the Fields
The Diary of Ruth's Fellow Harvester

The author would like to thank everyone at Educational Publishing Concepts, the team at Baker Publishing Group, and Tina Novinski.

To my sister, Tina Novinski, and my children, Michal Tyra
and Alexandra Tyra:

Come to the edge, Life said. They said: We are afraid. Come to the edge,
Life said. They came. It pushed Them . . . And They flew.
—Guillaume Apollinaire

© 2005 by Baker Publishing Group

Published by Baker Books
a division of Baker Publishing Group
P.O. Box 6287, Grand Rapids, MI 49516-6287
www.bakerbooks.com

Printed in the United States of America

Library of Congress Cataloging-in-Publication Data

Adams, Anne, 1645-
    Songbird of the Nile: the diary of Miriam's best friend, Egypt 1527-1526 B.C./[written by Anne Tyra Adams.]
        p. cm. — (The Promised Land diaries ; 5)
    Summary: Living in Egypt in 1526 B.C., twelve-year-old Laila keeps a diary that describes the lives of her Jewish family and neighbors, including that of her best friend Miriam's baby brother, who comes to be raised by an Egyptian princess and is named Moses.
    Includes bibliographical references (p.).
    ISBN 0-8010-4525-8
    1. Miriam (Biblical figure)—Juvenile fiction. 2. Moses (Biblical leader)—Juvenile fiction. [1.Miriam (Biblical figure)—Fiction. 2. Moses (Biblical leader)—Fiction. 3. Jews—History—To 1200 B.C.—Fiction. 4. Egypt—History—Eighteenth dynasty, ca. 1570-1320 B.C.—Fiction. 5. Diaries—Fiction.] I. Title.

PZ7.A1974So 2004
[Fic]—dc22
                                          2004054736

Series Creator: Jerry Watkins and Educational Publishing Concepts, with Anne Tyra Adams
Cover Illustrator: Donna Diamond

The biblical account of Miriam can be found in the Bible's Old Testament book of Exodus. While these dairies and the epilogue are based on this and historical accounts, the character of Laila, her diaries, and some of the minor events described are works of fiction.